SCATTER

Mindy Macfarlane

ISBN-13: 9798867024857
ISBN-10: B0CN6WBDX6

Cover design by: Mindy Macfarlane
Library of Congress Control Number: 2018675309
Printed in the United States of America

CONTENTS

CHAPTER ONE:
SCATTER

"Hey mom, I'm on my lunch break, can I call you back later?"

"No, it's important, don't hang up!"

"What's going on, is everything okay?"

"Everything is fine. I just don't know what to get your father for Christmas."

"Jeez mom, you had me worried there for a second. I don't really know what to get him either. You know I usually just give everyone a gift card."

She laughed, "I was listening to a podcast earlier today and they said that gifts are more meaningful if they're experiences rather than physical things, like a trip to the theater or whatever. The memory of the experience will be appreciated more than another necktie or bottle of cologne."

"That makes sense, I have some nice memories of visiting the city museums with Lauren when we first started dating, although I have a feeling that dad wouldn't appreciate it as much as I did."

"I really wish you would've stayed in art school."

"Please mom, not this again."

"I'm sorry, it's just... anyways, what are you having for lunch?"

"The guys and I stopped by Tony's for pizza. Lauren stayed behind, she said she needed to catch up on some work project that our supervisor had assigned to her a while back. Pretty sure it's overdue by now."

"Oh yeah? How's she doing?"

"Other than falling behind on the project, she's doing really good. She's got some friend thing going on this weekend, a baby shower, I think. We're both doing really good, mom. We're looking forward to seeing you and the rest of the family next month. I've already picked up gift cards for everyone and she's going to make some Christmas cupcakes to bring over."

"That sounds great, Russ. Try to think some more about what I can get for your Dad, text me some ideas and I'll talk to you later. Tell Lauren I said hi!"

...

The overhead security footage shows the minutes leading up to Laurens death.

12:29 PM

We see Lauren inspecting the metal tube that is locked into the lathe. The lathe is off. She is wearing safety goggles and a form fitting work shirt, as is company procedure. When she turns the motor on, the headstock begins to spin. A cutting tool is already grasped firmly in her hand, she goes to move it towards the spinning metal, but then pauses and puts the tool down. She walks closer to the left of the lathe and reaches over, it seems that something has caught her attention from behind the security camera's view. As she reaches around to get a better look, a long chain necklace falls out from under her shirt, which was previously tucked inside her collar. It lands directly onto the moving spindle.

She's broken the most important rule when working at a factory- never get complacent around the machinery. All safety regulations are written in blood.

Her necklace wraps around the lathe and quickly starts to choke her. Her hair also gets caught up and tangles around the chain, strengthening its hold so she can't break free. Visibly panicked, she tries to push away from the machine as it pulls her head in closer. She flails her arm, grabbing for the EMERGENCY BUTTON, but her finger slips just out of reach. This all happens in less than two minutes. She tries to scream out for help but it comes out silent, no words can escape her strangled throat. The chain is locked tight around her neck as the spindle continues to drag her further in. Screaming wouldn't have done much good anyways, as there are no other coworkers around. It's a small department and they've all gone off to lunch.

Lauren's head goes under first. She rips away with all of her strength but it's no use. The engine was built to counter resistance. There is no resistance as her skull is being crushed. A crunch can be heard over the rumbling of the machinery.

12:31 PM

The machine swallows the rest of her up in an instant, chewing and breaking every bone, grinding her up into a tenderized meat jelly.

Immediately flattening all of her vital organs until they burst.

Shredding away chunks of flesh until the concrete floor below her is *coated in blood, shiny and slick.*

And pulverizing each individual bone, from shin, to ribcage, to shoulder blade.

Instead of a dignified death, it does not spit her out intact. Her mangled corpse is stuck, hair and arms coiled up deep in the gears, clenched tight by metal jaws. She loops around over and over again to the indifference of the machine. The lower part of what's left of her body slams hard onto the concrete floor, each time scraping down her legs and feet just a bit further to their exposed bones. After a few rotations, a long dark streak starts to form on the ground, now saturated with her remains. Blood sprays out of her- into the air, onto the wall behind her, creating an opaque blur of red mist.

The lathe and her meld together as one. A dance of machinery and bone.

Flesh, breath, blood.

Steel, steam, oil.

You can briefly see the whites of her teeth peeking out through the dark red carnage freshly painted across her face, right before her head completely detaches itself from the rest of her body and gets sucked inside the inner workings of the lathe. Blood and brain drench the spindle as her headless body continues to spin around wildly, a beat up ragdoll in the grasp of a manic toddler.

12:33 PM

After a few more rotations, dangling pieces of her body begin to whip off of the rushing metal loop, and the rest of her skin rips open due to the sheer force of gravitational pull. Various organs and intestines, both large and small, are flung out in every direction before ending up scattered across the floor. What's left of her mutilated body continues to spin, mostly exposed skeleton at this point. A jagged bone sticks out from where her leg used to be. The ragdoll has lost all of its stuffing. This is the moment her coworkers return back from lunch.

...

The smell hits me before I can even comprehend what's happening. The strong smell of copper and raw meat. It's the scent of a slaughterhouse. Others raced around me in a frenzied panic but I could not move. I stood there, useless, frozen in place. Completely paralyzed. Unsure of what exactly I was staring at, at first.

This couldn't possibly be real. No. Maybe if I closed my eyes, I would snap out of it and the day would continue on as normal. All I have to do is finish up my work, clock out and drive home. Free to enjoy the rest of the evening just as I had done a thousand times before. I'd have a relaxing and normal night, everything would be fine. Everything is fine. Everything is fine. Everything is just fine.

I opened my eyes back up, but I was still standing there.

My wish had not been granted. Nothing will ever be fine again.

Now, everything that was happening around me, happened in slow motion. Everything moved as if underwater. I was far away and so cold. Freezing. This must be what shock feels like.

My mind was far away from the smells. The sounds.

Far away from the factory.

Far away from the chunks of disemboweled limbs and guts strewn about under my work boots.

Someone hit the emergency button as I continued to stand there, mouth gaped and wide eyed, still a million miles away. The lathe powered down and as it did, the sound of the body bashing onto the floor slowed down as well, each heavy thump quieter and spread out longer than the last, until everything stopped.

What little of the body that was left hung down from the spindle. The mass of remains did not resemble anything remotely human. I could barely make out half a leg, an arm and a torso.

Her torso.

Her torso that I had held from behind as we stood in our kitchen this morning. We talked about weekend plans while she drank her coffee and laughed. Her torso.

A sharp pain shot up into my hands and knees- I had collapsed onto the floor without even knowing, the weight of what just happened had fully hit me. A gut punch that knocked me to the ground. Coworkers gathered around me, they picked me up and quickly rushed me away from the scene. One or two whispered quick condolences, others shook their heads or buried their faces into their hands. I was guided towards the break room by my supervisor. He wore a plaid shirt.

Before we reached the break room, I stopped walking and screamed. A primal kind of wail that I had only previously heard made by wild animals when they're dying.

Lauren was dead. My wife was dead.

I've never seen the security footage. I don't need to. Every time I close my eyes I see it. Over and over and over again.

CHAPTER TWO: STIR

It's been about a week since Lauren's funeral. Most of her family had already left our town except for her older brother Brian, and his fiancée, Jennifer. Although Lauren and I had been married for almost seven years and I had spent plenty of evenings with him during family holidays and get-togethers, Brian and I weren't very close. Nothing against the guy, we just didn't have much in common. He was a sports guy and I was... not. They were staying with me and had offered to help- to cook and clean and get things sorted while I grieved. Although I was grateful, I was beginning to need my own space back. That clear headspace that only solitude can bring. I wasn't sleeping at all and I hoped once they left I would eventually fall back into some semblance of normalcy. Whatever "normalcy" meant after becoming a widower.

Every night when I closed my eyes and tried to sleep, all I could see was Lauren wrapped up in the lathe, screaming out for help.

I went over it in my head. I had been at that factory for five years and had gotten her the job there, a little over a year ago. She had quit her previous position as a department store manager over some workplace bullshit that she wanted no part of. Now I'm here, alone, cursing God and just wishing I could go back and fix everything.

"C'mon babe, it'll be great!" I told her, "The money is good, we can drive up together and you'll pick up the basics in no time."

She could be with me right now. Alive.

Fuck.

I kicked my nightstand and threw a stupid hardcover book across the room. It knocked my alarm clock off of the dresser before landing on the floor, face down, beside her sneakers.

"Please God, please. Let me go back to last week. It was just a week ago. Let me warn her. It shouldn't be like this. She should be here. She was just here. This doesn't make any sense..."

"Russell, come downstairs if you want, Jen made dinner." Brian called up to me from the dining room.

I was wearing the same clothes as yesterday and had barely left my bedroom upstairs. The days and nights were starting to run together. Without work, time had lost meaning. Without my better half, life had lost meaning. I had not showered nor shaved. My hair was greasy. My eyes, tired and dark. Her closed casket funeral had taken its toll on me, and I had aged considerably in a week.

Brian and Jennifer were sitting at the dining room table where Lauren and I used to sit every night. Photos of us hung on the wall behind the table. A wedding photo. A day at the beach. A caricature of us that we posed for while we were visiting the state fair.

A casserole dish full of baked lasagna was on the table.

"It still doesn't seem real, none of this," I looked at the stairs behind me, "I felt like she was going to be right there, following me down."

"I know, Russell, I know."

"If there's anything you need. Anything at all."

I sat down and joined them at the table, saying nothing.

This past week I had only eaten to keep myself alive. Food wasn't enjoyable any more, it was only sustenance. Everything was bland but necessary.

I held up a piece of lasagna with my fork, and a string of cheese pulled long and thin, mixed with warm chunks of meat and sauce. It clung to the plate and I shoved it into my mouth. It twirled around on my fork and hung from my lips.

Some time passed. We made polite small talk.

Something about a football game. Something about the cold weather. A new movie that just came out. A neighbor's dog. Their garden. Jen's mom. Something something. Static. I tried to follow along but nothing they said made any sense. I don't think I was making any sense either. It was all just distant noise to me.

The lasagna had begun to cool off.

It was now cut up into shreds, cold and rubbery. Gooey cheese had begun to coagulate and the ground up beef was picked apart and strewn around. No longer neat and orderly, the whole thing had fallen apart, only held together by a cold thin layer of chunky tomato paste. Stringy pasta was splattered up the sides of the casserole dish.
A red bloody mess.

It started to resemble something.

Lauren's eyeball appeared in the mess. It looked back at me.

I wasn't hungry anymore.

"Hey, listen, you guys have been really amazing. Thank you so much for staying with me and helping me through all of this. I know you have to get back to your jobs and life and everything. I... I think I'll be okay for now."

"Are you sure?"

"We're here for you, we can stay longer."

"No, really, I'll be okay," I lied.

"Call us if you need anything."

The only thing I needed was for everything to be different.

They wished me well, packed their bags and off they went. When I was sure they were gone, I let out a deep sigh. And then I was alone. Alone in my house for the first time, ever. There was an emptiness inside of me that I had not felt in a very long time. And back then, I had hope. Youth and dreams and ambition. Now, almost two decades later, I have nothing. I have emptiness plus time. The rest of my life.

Where do I go from here?

...

My house was filled with heaps of fresh bouquets of flowers from her funeral. Roses and lilacs and orchids.

My house was filled with heaps of dirty piles of unfinished labor. Laundry and dishes and unopened mail.

The duality of grief.

Both heaps equal in suffocating me. Every corner was a stark reminder. Every table was full of memories. Her white coffee mug with her lipstick still imprinted on the side, her reading glasses next to it. It was like she was just in another room, but always out of reach.

Her cell phone rang. Another telemarketer. I thought Jen had canceled all of her subscriptions.

"She's not here. She's gone. She's dead. And I'm sick of fucking telling you people that. Stop fucking calling."

I stomped past a pizza box that was on the floor. There was still pizza inside. Mold was starting to form on the glasses and bowls in the sink. Gnats were everywhere, and anytime I did gather the strength to throw something away, dozens of them would swarm up from the trash can. They crawled around on the food left out on the counter, and collected in the corners of the ceiling. I couldn't get rid of them all. I didn't care anymore, I didn't give a fuck about any of it. Bear witness to the lowest moment of my life.

I screamed at God but he didn't acknowledge me.

The days all blurred together, one by one until I couldn't distinguish one week from the next. The sky was blue, the sun shined bright. Neighbors laughed in their yards outside. Birds chirping in the early morning. The world kept going on without her.

The world spins and spins.

My living room felt smaller, the whole house felt smaller. And suddenly I was an unwelcome guest in my own home. *Persona non grata.*

The walls were closing in on me. This room was going to suffocate me. The walls were going to crush me. I paced around my shrinking home. It was so small and unfamiliar and alien that I wanted to throw up.

What if I insisted she come to lunch with us? What if I stayed behind with her? I could've stopped the lathe before it killed her. Maybe she would've just lost an arm.

I stared out the living room window for a long time. Uninterrupted hours of time. Families walked by on the sidewalk. Walking their dogs. Babies in strollers. Life had different plans for me. I laid down on the couch and closed my eyes.

Her body spun and spun.

I have to get out of here. I couldn't be in this house a day longer.

...

Inside of my closet was a Christmas present that I had bought for Lauren a few weeks prior. A KitchenAid mixer, boxed up in red and green festive wrapping paper with a shiny bow on top. She enjoyed baking in her free time, a longtime hobby of hers. She even sold her baked goods for special events- birthday parties and bridal showers. Cakes and muffins, cookies and banana bread. Her specialty was German chocolate cake. We watched baking shows together and she dreamt of competing on them one day.

I held the box in my arms and rested my head on top of it.

Outside of the house, snow began to fall. A drop in temperature soon followed. The remote to the television was lost, and after searching for too long, I finally found it buried beneath one of the many piles of accumulated junk.

"We here at Local 65 have been tracking this upcoming storm. Here's Mary with the latest report:"

"It's the first snowfall of the season and it's going to be a big one! This storm will produce heavy snow, powerful winds and blizzard-like conditions throughout the east coast. It will rapidly intensify by the morning and into the afternoon. There is a snow storm warning in effect starting at 3am tomorrow. Right now the temperature is 23 degrees and dropping, Brrrr! It's getting cold out there guys! Better pull out your winter coat if you haven't already! The snow clouds are already showing up on our radar. This massive storm could deliver more than two feet of snow and will move up from the east coast as the day progresses. Please prepare accordingly- stock up on groceries, especially batteries in case of power outages, and please do not travel."

I needed to get out of here before I got trapped inside. I couldn't breathe anymore.

I pulled a suitcase from the closet and hurriedly packed it, but I couldn't figure out where I wanted to go. I just knew that I needed to leave. I needed something to get my mind off of everything. I don't know. Some dumb distraction. Anything before I get swallowed up in grief completely.

What I really needed was a good night's sleep. At night I would reach out to grab her and be met with the truth all over again. Maybe I could trick myself into sleep if I could just get a change of scenery. A different room. A different bed. Tell myself that I'm on vacation and that she is at home waiting for me. There was a crisp coldness in the air, so crisp you could feel a sharpness in your lungs when you inhaled.

I got into my car and drove off. I made my way onto the highway and just kept driving. Autopilot had set in, no destination in sight. I just kept driving.

CHAPTER THREE: SIBERIA

On the highway, only a few cars drove past me, each driving with intent, some needed purpose or emergency. That was the only explanation as to why they'd be caught up along with me in this impending storm. Each lone car on the highway had a different story to tell. The trees on either side all blurred together, dark bare branches that twisted against the winter sky. The highway itself was rhythmic and hypnotizing, painted yellow lines that stretched on forever.

I'd been driving for a few hours already at this point. All of the radio stations were unfamiliar, far from my local signal, gone way past its reach. I was in another state by now, I think? Surely I had to have been. A song came on that I loved, it reminded me of summer vacations and better days. I turned it off and drove in silence.

Another hour went by and the sky had really opened up, spilling out dense white blankets of snow. Big white flakes lit up by my headlights. Night had approached long ago and I still had no clue where I was going. As I drove, the light poles kept coming. Electric saviors guiding me to an unknown destination. Statuesque angels with bright halos that beckoned the weary traveler. My road trip to nowhere.

"REDWOOD MILLS- GAS STATION 2 MILES" the large green sign said in big white letters.

I steered right, taking the exit ramp off of the highway and onto the next route, making my way into the rest area town. It was an urban hellscape of concrete, billboards and telephone wires. I was in the right place.

The gas station I stopped at was nothing out of the ordinary.

I picked up some snacks and an energy drink to keep me awake. The flavor of the energy drink was unlike anything found in nature. Should I stay in this rest stop town for a little while longer or should I find a motel?

As I wondered, the snowfall grew heavier than it had all night, obstructing my view. The weather had made the choice for me.

The snacks were long gone when I realized that I was still hungry. Before I found a motel or whatever, I needed to eat something filling, something starchy. I don't know what I was thinking, I should've gotten an actual meal hours ago. That's the problem, I wasn't thinking. I couldn't think. It was past four A.M. and all of the restaurants were closed. The snow continued to fall. The white flurries on the road danced and swirled like thrown powder underneath my tires.

Jesus Christ Russell, what the hell are you even doing out here? What the fuck were you thinking? Where the fuck can I get some God damn food?

I considered turning back.

I considered speeding up and driving my car into a tree.

Just when I had run out of ideas, I saw a 24-hour diner in the near distance. Salvation.

The bright neon sign read:

"SHIRLEY'S DINER – Get Stuffed!"

The diner was something out of the ordinary.

The building was painted in hot pinks and pastel greens, the inside matched in color. Pepto-bismol pink walls with seafoam green trim all around, and not at all appetizing. Bright cartoon stickers were plastered on the front entry doors. Plastic dolls, toy cars and action figures lined the ceiling, superglued down in place. A mosaic of everyones' childhood bedroom scattered about in an orchestrated mess. The music was loud, grating and like nothing I ever listened to. A hostess whose hair matched the walls greeted me and led me to a table.

I didn't have the mental capacity to deal with this, but I didn't really have a choice. No other places were open and I just needed something in my stomach.

"Howdy! Welcome to Shirley's. Here's the menu, pumpkin. You been here before?"

"No."

The waitress was wearing a purple and pink polka-dotted print cardigan and eyeglasses that were long and pointed at the sides. Her hair was up in a tight bun and her arms sported more tattoos than bare skin.

"Okay so, right now we're only doing breakfast. This morning's special is pancakes and grits"

I had never had grits before.

"Can I get you started with a drink?"

I just needed something starchy and I guess pancakes were a safe bet. You can't really fuck up pancakes.

"I'll take a coffee. I'll get the pancakes too, thanks."

"Sure sugar, be right up."

I passed the time staring at the assortment of children's playthings that decorated the walls and ceiling. The music continued, obnoxious and spastic, throbbing beats that I couldn't tune out. What would Lauren think of this diner? She enjoyed places like this, with all their quirks and charm, but she was also quick to roll her eyes.

I wondered what her last thoughts were, if she knew that that moment was going to be the end of her life. Her last conscious actions on earth. I hope she went quickly, that she didn't suffer. I hoped that if there was an afterlife that she was at peace right now and I hoped that wherever she was, the music was better.

Is this enjoyable music? Do people really like this? It was hard to comprehend, being almost 40 and not having stepped into a nightclub in almost twenty years. Everything in this moment felt so foreign to me. The music, the waitresses' outfits, the ironic decor.

The need to get away from my home was overwhelming. The only problem with running away from everything was that no matter where you go, you are still there. You can't escape yourself. That inner monologue inside of your head that holds you down under the heavy weight of your own introspection. You can't ever truly outrun who you are. I'm Russell. I'm 38 years old. I'm a widower. I hate this place.

The waitress came back with my coffee while I continued to stare off, ruminating in my thoughts. I stirred the full mug around a few times without drinking any of it, watching the black coffee and cream swirl together when she decided to interject.

"You okay, teddy bear?"

"Yeah, I'm alright, I just have a lot on my mind. I've had a long day. I've been on the road all night and I'm starving."

"Oh, you're not from around here? What brings you to Redwood?"

"I don't know" I took a sip of my coffee, "I just need a distraction."

The waitress nodded and told me she'd be back soon with my pancakes and grits.

While I waited, a plastic ballerina stared at me from across the room. A pale rocking horse grinned in the corner. A miniature train buzzed above me, the tracks built high into the ceiling, with a tiny garden gnome as its conductor. Anywhere I looked, dozens of bright happy toys looked back. Mocking me and my grief with their candy coated surrealism.

The snow continued to fall outside, snowflakes illuminated white by the waning moonlight and street lamps.

The waitress came back and set the plate of pancakes down on my table with a small bowl of grits on the side. A happy face was drawn on the pancakes in whipped cream.

I must've made some kind of face, because she stopped in her tracks to acknowledge it.

"What's wrong? You said you needed a distraction."

She flashed her best customer service smile.

I didn't reciprocate.

"Should I take them back and bring you some sad face pancakes instead?"

"No, no, it's fine. Like I said, I'm just having a rough day. I don't even know where I am. I drove out here on a whim."

"Hmm. Well, you happen to be in luck. Redwood Mills is a touristy place, there's plenty to do around here, even in the off season." She paused, "There's an indoor water park nearby, although that's more for the kids, a mountain trail with a bed and breakfast about half an hour away and a casino resort just north of here."

"I don't know. It's a bit snowy for a hike and I'm not really much of a gambling man."

"What about the water park?"

I shrugged my shoulders. "I didn't pack my swim trunks."

"Well, I'm sure you'll find something to do. I'll be back soon with more coffee."

The pancakes were doughy in the middle. I guess it was possible to fuck them up.

While eating, I reconsidered going to the casino. The lights and sounds could be a nice escape for a little while. Hell, maybe I could even win a few bucks. I tried the grits but the texture was mushy and unpleasant. I sloshed it around and swallowed it anyway. The waitress came back with more coffee and I told her that I'd changed my mind and would head to the casino after all. She gave me some rough directions on how to get there, a place called The Lucky Owl.

"I like card games. Blackjack and poker are my favorites." She lit up.

"I don't even know how to play," I replied.

"You've never even played poker before, really?" her voice raised a little, almost animated.

She continued, "Okay so, poker is easy. Each round you make a bet if you think your cards are better than the other guy's cards. There's different hands you can get dealt, like a straight flush or a full house." She pulled out her phone and looked up different winning combinations to show me, "For example, a full house consists of..."

As she continued explaining the game, another table got her attention and off she went, leaving me surrounded with all of the plastic dolls on the wall. Just me and the dolls, with their big vacant eyes.

I could see the rays of dawn were starting to break the sky through sticker covered diner windows. Slits of sunlight rested on my table. The snow continued to fall but it had let up a bit, it was probably a lot worse back home. I checked my phone and it was just before 6am.

I got in my car and headed north, leaving the uncomfortable whimsy of the diner behind.

CHAPTER FOUR: STAY

To get to the resort, the waitress told me, I had to drive down a secluded pathway off of the interstate. It was hidden by a wooded area of bare trees and not much else. Not exactly a forest, but close enough. Once I passed the wooded area, I'd come up to a boardwalk, parallel to the ocean. She told me that since it was the off-season, there wasn't much activity happening there, but that the casino itself should be pretty busy.

As I made my way down the winding path, the quiet reprieve of nature was interrupted with the juxtaposition of a huge, lavish building, nestled in between the end of the wooded area and the beginning of the coastal town. A giant neon cathedral that separated the forest and the ocean from one another.

I had never visited a beach in the winter time, and seeing snow instead of sand against the ocean struck me in a funny way that I wasn't expecting, an odd sort of nostalgia for a place that I had never been to before. I could also see the parking lot for the casino resort up ahead, and I was surprised to see it absolutely packed with cars. Not a soul was on the boardwalk however, and most of the shops along the way looked boarded up and closed for the season.

A giant golden statue of an owl with tall skinny legs and a king's crown atop its head greeted me as I drove up to the parking lot. It held out a large wooden sign that was intricately decorated, ornate with painted cursive letters and flourishes. It was out of place and weirdly inviting.

THE LUCKY OWL
CASINO RESORT
ENJOY YOUR STAY

As I neared the building, a group of vultures had gathered around the middle of the parking lot, picking apart the carcass of a freshly wounded opossum that appeared to have been dragged from the wooded pathway to the lot, with a wet trail of blood following behind it. I thought it was odd to see vultures so late in the year, especially with how cold it had gotten. But I didn't think too much of it.

Some vultures were circling overhead but most were on the ground, tearing the roadkill apart. They pecked away at its fat belly, its matted fur and pelt spread out over a flurry of sharp claws and light snow. The opossum's entrails spilled out over the pavement and steam rose from the warm gaping hole in its stomach. Two vultures tugged away at the same long intestine, caught in the middle of a slippery game of tug of war. They flapped their wings and hissed while digging their beaks deeper into the guts of the vermin.

They say when a group of vultures are feeding, it is called a wake. Some say it appears as if the vultures are mourning the dead, their heads bowed low, solemnly gathered around the body. But there was no respectful mourning taking place here. They were just opportunistic scavengers rejoicing in their newly acquired fortune. Happy. Filled with meat and fat. Not everything has to be poetic.

Even in the early morning hours, the lobby was operating like it was a busy Saturday night. Groups waited on bulky velvet couches that looked like relics from the nineteen seventies. A line of people led up to the front desk to check in. The elevator to the right stayed in motion, letting guests on and letting guests off. Well manicured plants were placed strategically around the room, next to tables and chairs, so green and perfect they appeared artificial. There was a mounted deer head above the desk that looked down at the lobby and everyone in it.

The walls were a deep oxblood red and brocade or damask in pattern, I could never figure out a way to tell the difference between the two. Floor-to-ceiling curtains draped the windows, a few shades darker than the crimson walls that surrounded me, and they didn't allow any light in at all.

Above my head hung ivory-colored chandeliers, thin and delicate. As I looked closer at their detail, I realized that they were carved from bone. They were actual ivory, not just in color. At my feet laid a dizzying sprawl of carpet, its pattern too disorienting to possess a name.

Even with all of the light fixtures, the building still seemed so dimly lit. It could've been any hour. Any season. An indefinite period suspended in time, never moving forward or backward. The lobby was at a standstill with a timeline that stayed in place. It contradicted everything we're taught about. Those W questions. Who? What? Where? **When?** Why? The whole thing was aesthetically hazardous. An anachronism in the middle of a quiet coastal town.

An older man walked past me pushing a trolley, it held a large aquarium that was covered up with a wool blanket. I could only see the bottom of the aquarium where the blanket didn't reach. It was filled with pale green gravel, the kind you would find at a pet store. Another man followed behind him holding two small cages in each hand, a turtle in one and a small pair of iguanas in the other.

Next to the front desk, a shelf of pamphlets displayed all of the attractions in the area. Coupon books. Local magazines. Menus. Museums. A glossy flier advertising the indoor waterpark that the waitress had mentioned. There was a guide for the resort among everything else on the shelf. I picked it up and flipped through it, noting the number of shops and restaurants residing inside. This place was so much bigger than I had envisioned, than what the waitress had made it seem with her off-handed suggestion. I've been to plenty of hotels in my lifetime, sure, but this was a whole different experience. This was a shopping mall.

There was a directory on the last page of the guide. "A fucking map, seriously?" I said out loud.

While in line to check in, I heard a muffled song, a ringtone, most likely coming from the cell phone of the man who was standing in front of me. It was a classical song, that I could tell, and it was one I was very familiar with. It was a song I knew quite well. The man didn't answer it. He didn't even take it out of his pocket to see who it was.

"Vivaldi?" I asked

He turned around and glanced at me. "Hmm?"

"Winter, by Antonio Vivaldi? Your ringtone." I asked again while pointing at his pocket.

"What? No, I don't know what you're talking about." He turned back around.

After checking in for the week, I decided I would go straight to my room and try to sleep before exploring the resort. God knows I needed it. Hell is a road trip with no destination in sight and I had been in my car with the devil for eight hours straight.

"DING."

The elevator doors opened up and I wheeled my suitcase inside. A woman was sitting on the elevator floor, her back to me and facing the wall, her head in her hands.

"I lost it all. He took everything. He cheated! He's a swindler!" She shrieked to no one, her head still buried. "He took it all."

"Are you okay?" I asked, not really wanting to know.

"No! I lost everything. I have nothing. It's all gone." She continued to cry into her hands.

"I'm sorry."

"Leave me alone. Go away! GO AWAY!" She demanded, while we were still halfway between floors with barely six feet of space between us.

I decided it was in my best interest to not engage with her anymore. She continued to scream at the wall and I backed up into a corner.

"The silk, the fabric was so bright, it was blinding." She screamed at me, this cryptic message that I didn't understand yet.

She then lifted her head from her hands, turned around and looked up at me. Where her pupils should have been were two milky clouds of thick cataracts instead.

"He took everything!" She got up in my face and gestured to her eyes, "He'll take everything from you too!"

She stopped screaming momentarily, but when she opened her mouth to scream again, the unsettling sound of what could only be described as the roar of a lawn mower engine exited her body instead; threatening, loud and vicious.

I felt the sides of my forehead turn hot with sweat, my stomach churned. I couldn't push her out of the way, even though I wanted to. If she were a man, I could at least shove her out of my face or even deck her if things went south, but I'm not trying to get kicked out of this place. I just fucking got here. It was such a small elevator, there was nowhere to go.

I was an animal stuck in a bear trap, wishing I could gnaw my own foot off to escape.

I planted my feet firmly on the ground, and pressed my body into the wall far away from her, trying to create as much space and distance myself from her as best as I possibly could in this cramped square shared between us.

She was still screaming at me, still shrieking at me with the strange intensity of lawn mower noises, this unthinkable, ungodly sound that humans weren't supposed to be able to make naturally.

All I could do was wait.

I had a therapist once, a few years ago. I don't really want to get into the details of why, but she taught me a technique that I could use to anchor myself down whenever I was feeling anxious. A breathing exercise to kind of center myself and regulate my emotions.

I needed to do that now.

Inhale.

One thing to smell – the stale, stagnant air inside the elevator.

Two things to touch – My suitcase, the resort guide.

Three things to see – The dandruff on the top of the woman's head, the phone number on the wall to call in case of an emergency and the elevator button that lit up white as it finally reached my floor.

Exhale.

"DING."

The hallway to my room stretched long and endless, an illusion of the carpet, which had the same dizzying pattern as the lobby. I walked past a fully stocked vending machine, and what appeared to be an empty conference hall. My room was at the far end of the hallway and on the left.

Inside, the bed was made, the sheets were crisp and there was generic art of blue flowers in a vase hanging on the wall. There was a mini fridge under a writing desk and a coffee maker on top of it. The lamps on the table were modern, the lampshades white. A television on the dresser. The carpet was clean and vacuumed. No dust, no stains. Everything in its right place. Nice and neat and orderly. There was no history here, just an infinite present.

I opened the curtains to the only window in the room. There was a dried up fly curled up in the corner sill. I pushed my pointer finger into it and its hollowed body crunched audibly beneath my fingernail.

CHAPTER FIVE: SPIRAL

Lauren and I are at our home, sitting on our living room couch. We are holding hands and facing each other. Her hands are soft and warm. I miss holding them.

"I don't want to do this, I'm scared," she whimpers. "I don't want to die."

There is an industrial sized lathe in our living room. It is loud and rumbling. I can feel the floor vibrating beneath my feet. I want to comfort her but when I open my mouth to speak, nothing meaningful comes out.

"It's going to hurt. There has to be some other way." She continues to tremble and I squeeze her shaking hands.

"I can't. I can't die now. I was excited about so many things. I just bought an ugly sweater to wear to Aunt Barb's Christmas party. I was going to make cookies shaped like reindeer. We had plans to go to the Outer Banks this summer, remember? I was looking forward to laying on the beach with you and watching the crabs scuttle by. Maybe we can still go?"

I squeezed her hands tighter.

"I don't want to die. I'm so scared. I thought we had so much more time left together."

She gets up from the couch and walks towards the lathe. I stand in front of her and hold her hands as tight as I can. She pulls away from me and continues onward as if under a spell. Her eyes glazed over, mesmerized by her impending fate. I beg her to stop, to sit back down and talk with me more. She slowly approaches the spinning lathe and sticks her hand in.

I woke up. Only an hour had passed.

I'm in my resort room, on the bed, laying on top of the covers. My jeans are still on. My shoes are still on.

The resort guide was still tight in my grasp.

I guess I'm not going to be getting a decent sleep here either.

Since I couldn't sleep, I decided to distract myself instead with this vast experience of consumerism outside of my resort door. The Lucky Owl had so much to offer, so much to do. I'd explore the building – check out the shops, and maybe the casino.

I sprinted past the elevator and decided to take the four flights of stairs down instead. They opened up right into the chaos of the main hall.

There was a bar that seemed pretty standard. It had a modern and welcoming vibe with a few people congregating around inside. They were watching a horse race that was playing on jumbo flat screen televisions above the bartenders' heads and some held numbered tickets in their hands. I also could see that the bar was fully stocked, its shiny black shelves full of expensive bottles of gin, aged whiskey, vodka and bourbon.

Further down, there was a spa that offered manicures, pedicures, massages and more. A massage sounded alright until I saw their prices listed.

I made note of a gift shop which could be useful, a convenience shop which would definitely be useful and an upscale boutique, which wouldn't be of any use to me at all.

There were three different restaurants – one looked like a typical casual dining restaurant, serving up burgers and pasta, while the one across from it was a fine dining place. A place that you'd want to be dressed up real fancy for, something exclusive for the members of a higher society. The third restaurant was a buffet, and I assumed the cheapest option. I figured that's where you ended up if you had lost all of your money at the casino. They each had different names but I wasn't really paying attention to their signs, it wasn't important.

Past the restaurants there was a small coffee shop, with tall flower pot vases on each side of the two door entrance. A sign that just said "Cafe" in a fancy but overused cursive font was hanging above the doors. I could remember that because how could you forget the name of a cafe when it is named "Cafe?" The aroma of rich espressos and freshly baked pastries drifted nearby, lingering in the air.

And next to that was where all the real excitement was. Next to the cafe was a huge spiral staircase that curved around and opened up to the casino on the bottom floor. The whole lower level was dedicated to the casino, which wasn't surprising considering that it was the main attraction and the reason why people were here.

All of this was inside of the resort. Everything. I didn't even have to leave the building. It was its own functioning ecosystem. A self contained neighborhood. But everywhere I went was dimly lit. Anywhere I walked, the maze-like whirlwind of clashing carpet and immaculate plants followed. ((((((terrium sentence))))))

The casino itself was unfamiliar territory to me, intimidating almost. It was something that I had only experienced previously through watching movies or playing gambling games on my phone. All around me were bright blinking lights and shrill buzzers that were designed to hit you right in that happy dopamine section of your brain.

The patterns on the walls and carpet clashed even more than the rest of the resort – bold jewel-toned shapes and spirals, purposely confusing and loud. Clocks nowhere to be seen. This was all meant to disorient a lesser man, but I was privy to their design. Everything has a purpose behind it, and once you start looking for meaning, things begin to make sense.

Somehow the whole atmosphere felt sleazy but elegant at the same time. Tacky but lavish. Gaudy and decadent and classy and stupid, like wealthy siblings fighting over their dead parent's estate. Or wearing an Oscar De La Renta suit to your parole hearing.

I observed a few rounds of high stakes poker but didn't join in, and after watching some big losses happen I realized it would be in my best interest to stick to the dollar slots.

Rows and rows of slot machines filled most of the casino space. Aisle after aisle of bright colors and flashing screens. Technicolor monoliths that would bestow you with riches or debt. And since these machines were not sentient, incapable of feeling sympathy or remorse, they were fine with dishing out debt left and right. Mountains of debt. They were mathematically and psychologically tuned to make each player lose their money slowly over time. That's what they were designed for, anyways, designed by people who maybe at one time still felt empathy or regret but not anymore. Everything that is not of nature is designed by man, but not all architects are created equal. Some are soulless.

There were slot machines of every genre imaginable – jungle themed machines with tigers and tropical birds, old west themed ones with cowboys and saloons. I sat down at a slot that had animations of spinning jesters and painted harlequins. It wasn't the classic 3-row type you'd typically imagine when you thought of these games. There were no cherries or bells here. Instead, on the screen in front of me were four lines, five rows and "1024 ways to play." It also featured free games, secret levels to unlock and bonus rounds. I had no idea what the fuck I was looking at. This was my first rodeo.

The first time I fed a dollar into the machine, some squares spun around and lit up. Then I did it again and new sound effects beeped and chirped. Maybe I was winning but I couldn't tell. I pulled the lever a few more times- more beeps and whistles, but it never did cough any tokens up.

In the aisle next to me, there was something going on. Something disruptive. A crowd had formed around two drunk men who were in each other's faces. They shouted and pushed each other as testosterone and spit flew between them. It seemed they were arguing over bets or drinks or a woman, who could tell? One guy was much bigger than the other and even though it didn't really matter, I was quietly rooting for the smaller guy. The underdog. Maybe he had started this whole encounter but I wanted to see him come out on top. Be victorious in the face of his goliath, this beast of a man who was currently screaming obscenities down at him.

The shorter guy had had enough and was now talking a big game. Hyped up on his own adrenaline and also possibly cocaine by the looks of it. I think he was trying to convince himself he could take this guy even if he was convincing no one else. He claimed that he was an MMA fighter, that he took on guys way bigger when he was in jail. He was definitely going to "beat this guy's ass" and that he was going to "fuck him up good."

A lot of big barking from such a little dog.

Things escalated when the underdog threw the first punch and barely fazed his opponent. The goliath reacted, his expression looked more amused than insulted by the attempt and he immediately threw the second punch. His punch landed. Hard. Right smack on the underdog's jaw, instantly knocking him out cold. The underdog's body crumpled and dropped, and when his head smacked the ground and bounced off, a few of his pearly white teeth flew out of his mouth. They rolled across the floor with a long glob of blood and spit following behind.

On the ground, his arms shot up and stiffened. His fingers twitched in the air. This is known as "the fencing response position." It's not uncommon to see in people who get knocked out, it means that they've suffered a concussion. At best.

Then the poor sap pissed his pants. Lights out, show's over. I hope he didn't have a wife or kids, because they will now be his caretakers. Or worse.

At this point security had shown up and dispersed the crowd. The goliath was escorted away and the underdog was left for the paramedics to deal with.

From bravado to brain-damaged.

No one else noticed this, but before the crowd had thinned out, I saw a shadow of a man sneaking his way over to the underdog's teeth. He bent down, picked them all up in one fell swoop and casually pocketed them all like he had done this a thousand times before. Then he disappeared back into the crowd.

Later that night, I watched this same strange man playing craps at a table. He was on a winning streak by the looks of it. The other players hooted and hollered, cheering him on like they were his own personal sycophants. He shook the pearly white dice and they flew out of his hands.They hit the table hard and rolled across the board.

But no glob of blood or spit followed them.

CHAPTER SIX: SOUVENIR

"Good morning, I'd like a large coffee please. No cream or sugar, I'll add it myself, thanks."

The cashier at the cafe handed me my coffee. The steam rose up to my nose and stayed there for a bit while I walked over to the other side of the cafe to fix up my drink and find a place to sit. The cup was too hot to hold without a cardboard sleeve around it but not so hot that I couldn't take a sip to taste it and make sure it was to my liking. It was.

I was beginning to settle into my new life at the casino resort.

I had awoken about an hour before in my hotel room, a ray of sunlight peering through the curtains and right into my still closed eyes. I had gotten two, maybe three hours of sleep which is much more than I had gotten in a while. I went to reach for Lauren out of habit but she wasn't there, obviously.

The room, the sun and myself minus everyone.

Back at the cafe, I poured a bit of cream into my coffee. There was a man next to me doing the same, while eyeing up the various pastries behind the display case next to the register. He had thinning hair, a bulbous nose and wore a work shirt with the words "Williams Auto Maintenance" embroidered onto the pocket. His teeth were yellow and cracked like rotted planks on an old wooden bridge. He decided on a donut.

He passed by me and said "hello" and on his way back we made some small talk. He seemed friendly enough, albeit a bit rough around the edges, but nothing new that I hadn't seen from my coworkers at the factory.

"I'm glad they're grinding the whole beans fresh today." He tells me in his southern drawl, "Last week the suppliers gave them pre-ground coffee and I can't drink pre-ground coffee. And I need my coffee, you know?" He chuckled.

"Why can't you drink pre-ground?"

"You see," He started, "When I was a little boy, I lived in terrible conditions with my mom and two sisters. Real poverty, you feel me? We didn't have hot water, sometimes no electricity, nothing. Place would get filthy 'cause we didn't have no money for cleaning supplies. It was a one bedroom apartment, my sisters and mom shared the room and I slept on the couch. Anyways, it was absolutely infested with cockroaches. They crawled on the counter top, crawled on me at night, under the blanket, in my clothes. When we were fortunate enough to have the electricity bill paid up, we would turn on the lights at night and they would scatter everywhere. Had to cover my toothbrush with plastic 'cause I caught one drinking the water off the bristles. One time a teacher, my favorite teacher, gave me a brownie and I was so happy, right? I ate half and put the other half in my pocket to save it for later. That's what you do when you're poor, 'cause you don't know when you'll eat again. I forgot about that brownie and I woke up to roaches swarming my pants. Like a big black squirmin' shadow in the dark. They were just all over me. So, not many people know this, but if you're around roaches long enough you can develop an allergy to them. And I did. You get all swollen and itchy, it's awful. I can only drink coffee that's been freshly ground. Can't drink the pre-ground stuff that they get delivered here or my throat will swell up."

"Oh. Huh." I said, when it finally clicked for me.

"Yup. I grew up poor as shit." He continued.

At this point I realized he was quite the talker, but I was okay with it. He was interesting, if nothing else. We walked over and took a seat on the retro couches in the cafe's lounge.

"One Christmas when I was twelve or so, my mom buys me a scratcher from the corner store, bless her. A fuckin' five dollar scratcher. Unheard of. I tell her to return it, I'd rather have a sandwich and a can of coke. But she insists. So, I shake my head and roll my eyes at her, and then I start scratchin'. Now, to win the jackpot, you gotta get three of them in a row. So, I'm scratching away, and I uncovered a jackpot... Then another!... then no more fucking jackpots." He laughs, a big hillbilly belly laugh.

"But then, get this- I scratched off the bonus section at the bottom and won a cool one hundred dollars. To a twelve year old me, that might as well have been the jackpot. It was a fuckin' Christmas miracle. I took the money and bought me and my sisters some presents. Got my mom a little necklace in a nice gift box too. Before they had even unwrapped them, I was already jonesin' for another scratcher. That's all it took. I was hooked. And here I am, forty some years later, still chasing that third jackpot. My white whale. What about you, what brings you here?"

"I just needed a distraction for a little while." I tell him and pause.

I realized that I couldn't match his long winded story telling and felt a bit anxious. I'm an inferior narrator, with nothing to say.

"I uh, my wife is, she's on a trip. For work. I needed to get out of the house, you know? It was just too quiet. I'm not much of a gambler but I didn't know what else to do with myself. So I took some time off of work and here I am, I guess."

"Well, mazel tov to that, my new friend." He holds his half empty cup in the air towards me in mock celebration. "I'm heading down to the casino soon, I'm sure I'll see you around."

He was right. I was back at the casino by lunch time.

The early afternoon crowd was different from the evening crowd. More drawn in, less happy. Most of them had dead eyes, glossed over and catatonic. Vacant eyes that were usually only seen in soldiers, mental patients and prostitutes. They were pulling levers not for fun but out of habit, like they had no other purpose in life. This was it, this was their calling. There was no excitement in their faces, it seemed to have been lost long ago. Their arms that pulled the levers appeared automatic, like robots programmed to do a single task. They were lined all in rows, dozens of rows, like assembly lines. Up and down, up and down. The air was thick with cigarette smoke even though smoking wasn't permitted inside the building. Winter by Antonio Vivaldi played on a speaker as I walked by. I stepped on something dense and sticky, gum probably?

Even amongst all the slot zombies, I felt better today. I was not one of them, my stay was temporary. A temporary respite, that would last a week long and not a day over. My kingdom for seven days of reprieve. Then I'd be back home. A good reset. A much needed break.

I sat down at a slot in the seventh aisle, twelve seats down. It was a forest creature theme. Deer ran on little squares, bears growled, foxes whipped their tails back and forth. I kept landing on owls and their heads would spin, but in a whimsical way, not a Linda Blair in The Exorcist kind of way.

This slot had a "scatter" feature. This feature is a bonus game, which locks you in once you hit four or more of the same "scatter" symbol on the reel. In this case, the symbol was an owl swimming in jewels. Once all four or more symbols appear, the machine would launch into a mini game where you can win more money. This machine's mini game was "free spins" and the owl would throw big handfuls of jewels at the screen. There was a small "paytable" icon that explained it all once I clicked it. I must have missed the icon in all of the confusion last night.

It took me a few rounds to understand, but it wasn't so complicated once I got the hang of it. I don't know why I felt so overwhelmed the night before. Beginner's anxiety, I suppose. First time jitters.

After playing many rounds, the scatter feature never did pop up, but some winning combinations did. The reel would stop and occasionally land on the right sequence, and when it did the machine would spit a few coins out. I think I was still in the red, but gaining something from doing nothing felt pretty alright. There is no way to make money by doing nothing at all, I thought. The only way to make money is to provide value. Was I providing value? Were all these zombies around me providing value? *Ex nihilo nihil fit.*

After a few more games, I was actually in the green, and had profited on a few bigger wins to my surprise. They came out of nowhere, just as easily as the losses had come last night. The technicolor monolith had deemed me worthy. I pulled the lever with promise and intent, my arm moved to a different beat than the others around me. My beginner's anxiety had turned into beginner's luck. Not a bad start to the day, I thought. I could get used to this.

I hauled my winnings to the bar upstairs and treated myself to a 6pm martini. On the left wall inside of the bar, there was pseudo-edgy artwork of a mean looking, ragged owl clutching a large gray rock in his talon, a bed of sparkling crystals laid beneath him-rubies, amethysts, black diamonds and emeralds. Why was the owl holding a rock and not one of the more expensive gems? It was a strange choice by the artist.

Other patrons at a booth next to me were deep in conversation when they invited me over. We shared stories and laughed amongst each other while the top shelf liquor continued to pour in excess. A man told a joke, an attractive woman told a better one.

"A horse walks into a bar," The man begins and is quickly interrupted.

"Why the long face? Everyone's heard that one, c'mon man." Says the interrupter.

"Shut up, shut up, let me finish." Says the first man in jest.

"A horse walks into the bar," He begins again, "and orders a rum and coke. This completely astounds the bartender. He's thinking "My God, a talking horse!" but then he says, "what the heck, I guess I might as well make him a drink." So he pours it and even garnishes it with a lime wedge, then he hands it to the horse. And wouldn't you know it, there's a twenty dollar bill on the counter. Now the bartender is really at a loss for words. A damn horse just walked into his bar, ordered a drink and then actually had a twenty dollar bill to pay for it. Still stunned, he takes the twenty and walks to the register to make change. While he's standing in front of the register he stops for a second and thinks to himself, "Let me try something here and see if the horse notices anything."

So he walks back over to the horse and hands him one dollar

in change. The horse doesn't say anything, he just stands there, sipping on his rum and coke. After a few minutes, the bartender can't take it anymore.

"You know," he says to the horse, "We don't get too many horses in here."

And the horse replies, "Well, at nineteen dollars a drink, I'm not surprised."

Everyone at the bar laughs at the man's joke. One guy exclaims he's heard it before but when he heard it, it was a gorilla, not a horse.

"I guess it could be any animal, really," says another.

"I don't think so, what about a crab?" The man jokes while his hands imitate that of crab claws, trying to grasp desperately at a drink in front of him. More laughs were had, including mine.

"He could use a straw!"

"No! His claws would cut the straw all up!" and he continued imitating claws, chopping an invisible straw to bits.

The attractive woman pipes up in between our laughter. "Okay, my turn, I got one."

She starts, "A beautiful woman is in a bar. She walks up to the bartender, extends her finger and seductively gestures that he should bring his face closer to her. As he did, she gently caressed his full beard.

"Are you the manager?" She asked, softly stroking his face with both hands.

"No," says the bartender.

"Well, can you get him for me? I'd like to speak to him." She said while running her hands beyond his beard and into his hair.

The bartender apologizes and says that he can't get the manager. "Is there anything I can do for you?"

She says "Yes. I need you to give him a message" and she runs her finger across his lip and slyly pops a couple of fingers into his mouth, and lets him suck on them gently.

The flustered bartender asks "What should I tell him?"

"Tell him," she whispers, "That there's no toilet paper, hand soap or paper towels in the ladies room."

The woman is done telling her joke and you can tell that she is pleased with her delivery. Around me, the whole bar is in fits of laughter. Someone in the crowd says "Hey now, some men pay extra for that!" and then comes more laughter. The whole mood is jovial and celebratory and good.

But in between these drinks and laughter, I started to feel something. A pang of new emotion, one I hadn't felt before. It was guilt. Here I am enjoying myself and laughing it up like a stupid drunk asshole with these strangers while my wife is fucking dead. She's dead and I am living and there is no rhyme or reason to it. She'll never get to laugh again. The hysterics of the crowd become loud and overbearing. They're hooting and hollering, slapping tables with wild looks in their eyes. There's a subtle sense of wickedness behind the raucous. The universe is mocking me. I feel the floor dropping. The mood of the whole bar shifts- the lights above me grow darker and the crowd's smiles twist upright. Their teeth bare wide in between the cacophony of laughter. Then all of their eyes turned on me. Staring.

I had told the universe I wanted to feel something other than sadness or anger and so it gifted me with a new emotion. The feeling of guilt was my souvenir.

I ran out of the bar and felt a nauseous spasm growing in my stomach. On my feet, I was in the throes of vertigo, induced by heavy intoxication. The carpet was an unsteady sea of mazes and each towering exotic plant I passed by was a ship I wanted to vomit in. Were there more plants out than yesterday? Why did the carpet feel even more dizzying? Was I seeing double? I was drunk and drowning on land. A labyrinth of hallways and judgment from an unseen God left me with nothing but a knot in my stomach, tied tight from guilt.

Guilt is a black dog that follows you. You can feel it behind you but when you turn around it's never there. It's just a feeling that always follows you but never presents itself tangibly. You can't touch guilt, or hold it, so you can't get rid of it, not in any physical way. It's just always there. That feeling. That pang in your stomach. A constant. And when you try to ignore it, when you push it down deep in the back of your thoughts and try to remain strong, you realize that it's not strength. It's a liability. It pulls you down with it. It owns you, it towers over you and you are at its mercy. And the dog is hungry. It's not a kind dog.

Back at the resort room, I tried to puke up my souvenir. The acidic taste burned my throat as it came up in buckets. I vomited so much there was nothing left but dry heaving, gagging and strained tears by the end. I didn't want it, this wretched, awful feeling- the universe can have it back. But it wouldn't leave me, the feeling of guilt would not leave my body. It was a gift that I couldn't return.

CHAPTER SEVEN: SCRUTINY

I woke up hungover as all hell. My bed spun beneath me until my eyes came into focus. My mouth felt dry like a thick piece of wool had been stuffed inside it, sucking any moisture up. And my head, my head just throbbed intensely. The room was impossibly bright. I got up, stumbled to the sink and downed a glass of water. Then another. It didn't help. A shot of whiskey or vodka was needed. Hair of the dog.

I was back at the slots and already into my third drink when the attractive woman from the night before approached me. She had on a thin white sweater that clung tightly to her body. Its v-shaped neckline was cut very low, but I didn't let my eyes wander. Her collarbones were peeking out, they were sharp, defined and appropriate to look at. She put her hand on my shoulder and I noticed that she was wearing a big diamond bracelet around her wrist.

"I hope you washed your hands," I said while smiling.

"Hmm?" She looked puzzled.

"Your joke, from the night before."

"Oh right, duh," she said, looking relieved. "You left kinda quickly last night, I didn't catch your name."

"Sorry, I wasn't feeling well. My name's Russell."

"Farrah" She motioned to herself, taking her hand off of my shoulder for a moment before resting it back there.

"You gonna be here for a while?" she asked me but I was too focused on the machine to give her a direct answer and just shrugged instead.

She kept talking to me but my eyes didn't meet hers, they were glued to the spinning slots. I was losing. Badly. I was hemorrhaging money. It was so easy to win yesterday, what was I doing wrong? What happened to my beginner's luck?

"Hmm," Farrah sighed. "It looks like you're not having much luck today."

I nodded my head, but I still wasn't giving her much of my attention.

She moved in closer, putting both hands on me, embracing me from behind.

She leaned down and whispered into my ear, "I can change that." her tone was sultry.

Oh. Is she flirting with me? No. No, she's an escort. Of course.

My words stammered out of my mouth, "Oh, um, uhhh sorry, I'm married. My wife is away on a trip, but when she comes home I'll be waiting for her." I held up my hand, pointing to my wedding ring.

"Well, if you change your mind and want to hang out later, I'm in room 429. I could really use the company." She smiled and sauntered away.

Later in the day I watched as the teeth stealing shadow man won round after round of blackjack. I picked up on the rules pretty quickly; the goal of blackjack is to get the closest to twenty one without going over. If you go over, you lose, it's called a bust.

The dealer dealt out cards to the players and the shadow man tapped his finger down onto the green felt table.

"Twenty one."

The dealer slid the chips towards him.

A new round.

"Twenty one."

and the dealer slides the chips towards him.

A new round.

"Twenty one."

And his crowd gathers around him.

It seemed statistically improbable. He had to have been counting cards or using some other means of cheating. The group continued to cheer him on. They grew larger in number, like locusts swarming around a field of crops. The swindler and his sycophants.

He always seemed to have a crowd around him, orbiting him. He must have a reputation of some kind here. Maybe he was from old money? The clothing and jewelry he wore suggested as much. It must be nice to have such a carefree life, to be able to gamble thousands away and gain your winnings back every time.

Why did God gift this man with charm and riches while cursing me with death and guilt? Don't I deserve a break? There was a lesson in there somewhere. The universe is as random as it is cruel.

The swindler continued to win round after round.

"Twenty one."

"Twenty one."

"Twenty one."

Did no one question this? He was chewing gum like an asshole while his sycophants carried on in celebrating his impossible winning streak. Classical music played softly over the speakers. Was it Vivaldi? Again??

I stared at the swindler's fingers, studying them, trying to catch him in the act. Not that I really knew what to look for. There was something strange about him. He looked like something that God drew with His left hand. He was built weird, lanky with a neck that was too long, but not long enough to notice unless someone pointed it out. The necklaces around his neck were bejeweled with gemstone pendants but he didn't strike me as feminine or an avant garde type. His short hair was soft brown and ruffled, and his nose was large and pointed, it took on an almost beaklike shape. His eyes, a dark brown, almost black. They didn't move naturally, instead they stared straight ahead and focused on wherever his head turned. When he spoke, he was charming and suave, a natural extrovert. But again, there was something wrong. Something off.

The image of himself that he wanted to sell to his cheering masses wasn't quite right, but they couldn't see what I could see.

The snake oil had venom in it.

His long fingers held the cards firmly. He chewed his gum and blew a bubble. When it popped, it was the only noise in the whole casino.

He never looked in my direction. I was just another face in the crowd. I have to admit, I felt small in his presence.

CHAPTER EIGHT: SQUIRM

By dinner time I had accepted defeat. After a day of losses at the slots I had to quit and recoup for the next day. Tomorrow will be better. I'll come out ahead. I walked down the endless hallway, overhead lights flickered above me and the carpet seemed to sway back and forth like calm waves, swirling in the ocean. There were more plants out now, larger ones, Monstera, Alocasia and Birds of Paradise plants with thick long vines and big round palm leaves at the ends of them which completely towered over my head.

The buffet upstairs was lacking in ambiance but had made up for it with its abundant selection of varied dishes. There was chicken and ribs and even a tray of shrimp. Other than that, it was mostly filler food like macaroni and cheese. Quantity over quality. No Michelin stars for this place, but for the price it didn't look half bad. I gathered a plate of food and sat down to eat. I was three bites in when I saw something skitter past my shoe and across the restaurant's floor.

It was the strangest insect I had ever seen. It was a centipede but... but it wasn't like any centipede I had ever found, not like the ones I've seen under rocks in my backyard or in my basement late at night. It didn't look native to the area, it looked like it belonged deep in the jungle, or some other tropical place. It was massive with a thick flattened abdomen that was entirely segmented. It had a bright red shell that was striped with hues of striking yellow- like a warning sign. And if the colors didn't warn you off, it had long sharp pincers that would. Its hundreds of legs scurried so fast across the floor and under another diner's table, that it disappeared before I could even register if it was real or if my eyes were playing tricks on me.

But I knew I saw it. It was unmistakably a giant fucking exotic centipede in a restaurant where I am currently having dinner.

Then I saw another.

They say that if you see one bug in your house, it's just one bug. But if you see more than one, you most likely have an infestation.

Were there more? Were they all crawling around in the kitchen? Scurrying inside ovens and atop silverware? Picking away at the buffet table, squirming their way inside the trays and pots of food, burrowing themselves in my pile of mashed potatoes? I pushed my plate away.

When the waitress came to check on me I gave her my full plate and told her I was done. No take out box needed, thank you. As I sipped on my glass of water and waited for the check, Winter by Vivaldi started playing again, but this time it wasn't quiet. It was booming. Full volume. Like an entire orchestra was three feet away from me. An army of shrieking violins, led by a crazed conductor.

No one else reacted to the cacophony of noise that had suddenly pierced through the entire room. What the hell was going on?

The music grew more intense, it was as if every single musician had sprouted extra arms that held another instrument, each one louder than the last. Violins and cellos that multiplied, escalating at every second with an ear splitting force of thunderous noise.

I couldn't take it anymore. I stood up and against my better judgment, I shouted. I wanted someone, anyone, to acknowledge this lunacy. To validate that I wasn't alone in this bizarre assault to my senses.

"DOES ANYBODY ELSE HEAR THAT? WHY IS CLASSICAL MUSIC EVEN PLAYING?? THIS PLACE SERVES FUCKING TATER TOTS FOR CHRIST'S SAKE."

The whole restaurant turned and gawked at me. A toddler in a frilly tutu started crying near my table while the mother tried to console her. "Shhh, shhh, it's okay. The scary man is just having a bad day. You're okay, everything is okay."

Humiliated, my face flushed over red and I took off to my room. It seemed like the only place in this whole Goddamn resort where I felt safe. I promised myself that I was going to leave this cursed place and go back home.

I would go back home as soon as I won my money back.

My room was clean, sterile. My clothes were folded neatly inside of the dresser. The towels and sheets had been replaced with new ones. A mint was left on the pillow. Inside the mini fridge, the shelves were stocked with small bottles of overpriced liquor- vodka, whiskey and tequila. I proceeded to drink them all. One after another- a race against the night.

I dug my fingers into my unwashed arms. Dead skin and sweat gathered underneath my fingernails. Dirt. Human clay.

Now blitzed out of my mind and on an empty stomach, I turned off the light and just laid in bed. Not sleeping, but not completely awake either. That in between phase where everything is warm and heavy but you haven't quite yet drifted off to dreamland.

Floating comfortably in a liminal, weightless existence. I gazed up at the ceiling fan and watched it go round and round. Next to the fan, there was a line in the ceiling that I hadn't noticed before. In the dark, it appeared to be a crack. And it seemed to be getting bigger.

There was a new and sudden danger above me but I was too shitfaced to do anything about it. I couldn't get up, I was so deep into the bed, the warm comfortable bed. My round belly swollen from liquor. Too apathetic to move. So, I kept a close eye on it. This increasingly growing crack above me.

There was a recent story in the news about a woman who watched a crack grow in her ceiling one night. She lived in an apartment complex near the Florida beaches. As she saw the crack get wider, her whole apartment began to shake and she quickly got out. Thankfully she escaped right before the whole building caved in. It was a monumental collapse caused by a sinkhole. It unfortunately took the lives of many of her neighbors. When interviewed, she stated that she got a gut feeling to get out of the building. It was instinctual, she claimed, something in her brain said "RUN NOW" and she listened to it.

Was I doomed to a fate of dying in a collapsing building because I was too drunk to try to run? Was this the end?

No really, I needed to take this seriously, I really should try to get up.

"Get up Russell, your sense of survival is abysmal. Come on, you dumb fuck."

The crack continued to grow longer and wider. Creeping ten feet above my head.

Fight, flight or freeze. You don't get to choose one, your instinct takes over and chooses one for you. My instinct wanted me dead. I froze and couldn't take my eyes off of it. A sober me would have had a better reaction I think, but right now I was confused and drunk and stupid.

The crack fell off and landed on my face.

It was not a crack in the ceiling after all, it was a big squirming exotic fucking centipede.

Before I could slap it off, it wasted no time and scuttled swiftly into my ear. It wiggled and thrashed around, trying to get in further, deep inside of my head. It sought a dark tight space to hide within, and quickly made itself comfortable.

"Oh shit, oh fuck, oh fuck, oh fuck ohfuckohfuckohfuckohfuck."

I turned the bathtub faucet on full blast and held my ear underneath the running spout, trying desperately to flush this thing out of me. It dug and scratched inside my inner ear canal, fighting against the rush of water. I felt every single leg, every writhing move it made as it buried itself deeper into my skull. Squirming violently against soft flesh and ear wax, crawling and scratching its way into the most vulnerable space of my body. Past tiny little bones and cartilage. An inch away from my brain.

Finally, after an unbearably, excruciating, disgustingly long time, it stopped wiggling. I had drowned it.

I now had two questions.

Is the convenience store on the second floor open?

Do they sell tweezers?

Down the hall my trip was quickly interrupted by a scene of pandemonium. Every door to a different room was wide open with maids furiously cleaning inside. Maids in the hallways. Maids on the stairs. Maids armed with bug spray, spraying the air thick with chemicals. A frightened maid shrieks loudly. More centipedes darted around me, across floors and walls. They were everywhere but barely visible, hidden in the swirling patterns of the wallpaper and carpet.

The walls were fully alive. Damask. Brocade. Centipede legs.

I made little notice of it, but there was a poster advertising an "Insect and Reptile Convention in the Conference Hall" that I quickly sprinted past. I kept up that sprint until I reached the convenience store. The door was locked and no one was inside.

"Open At 6am" the sign on the door taunted me.

"Fuuuck," I screamed internally. I just wanted this thing out of my head. I felt so gross, so violated.

I tried to drown out my feelings by screaming more internally. Internally as to not wake any sleeping guests in their rooms. Internally as to not embarrass myself again. I wanted to scream forever, but even your inner voice needs to stop to catch its breath. Go on, try it yourself. Let your inner voice scream and see how long it can last before it needs to stop and catch its breath. Why is that? Why does your internal monologue need to breathe? What else ticks inside of us that needs to come up for air?

"Did you know that the figure in Munch's 'The Scream' is not screaming, but is, in fact, reacting to hearing the scream?"

Who said that? Who the fuck just said that? The voice was so close, so intimate, it felt like it was coming from inside of my head but it was a voice that I was not familiar with.

In the lobby, The Swindler is awake. A few people crowded around him as he spoke. He's the center of the group, the center of attention, and he's talking about how his centipedes are on the loose.

"They wanted a taste of freedom and who am I to stop them?" he laughed. His audience was absolutely enamored by him, but to me, his mouth seeped like an opened wound. I wanted nothing more than to bandage it up. This was the first time I really listened to him speak, but there was a new familiarity in his voice. Wait.

The crowd returned his laughter, like cult followers swooning over their king. Their king of riches and lies. Of course the centipedes would be connected to him. His pets. I should have known. Filthy, disgusting little things.

The cafe didn't open for another hour, so I drank the coffee from the lobby's coffee maker. The pre-ground coffee. I sat at a distance from The Swindler and his sycophants. I stared at them. I'm seething but they don't take notice. I want to confront him. To confront him about releasing the centipedes and about his cheating at the blackjack table. To confront him for stealing the man's teeth off the floor, and stealing the sight from the angry woman in the elevator.

But he's surrounded by his sycophants. Always surrounded. There's safety in numbers. Now is not a good time to question him but I'll get to the bottom of this. Soon. I want answers but right now I have to wait. I have to be patient. Not patient like a saint, but patient like a sniper.

There are no clocks in the lobby. The floor beneath me is unsteady, an uneven terrain. The potted tropical plants are growing taller every day, like emerald green skyscrapers. The hallways seem longer and the lobby walls breathe with the souls of insects and con-men.

Life is a series of lobby rooms. Of waiting rooms. In between stages. You wait and wait in different rooms all of your life. You spend all of your days twiddling your thumbs and biding your time. Waiting. And then if you're lucky, you finally end your waiting one day, surrounded by friends and family. But you won't know it. Your final waiting room is a very small one once they close your casket.

The mounted deer head looks down and watches all of us closely. After some time, I made eye contact with The Swindler.

He's chewing gum. He talks to me from across the room. He doesn't open his mouth to speak but I can hear him clear as day. Telepathically. It's the same voice that spoke to me about 'The Scream' earlier and the same voice that talked about his centipedes on the loose moments ago. I don't know if anyone else can hear him, but no one else reacts, so I assume the conversation is just between us.

"When your wife's head went under and was crushed inside the machine, did it pop like this?"

He blew a bubble until it burst, then gathered it back in with his tongue.

"Fuck you!" I screamed, startling every single person in the lobby.

This was just the beginning. I could tell. This was going to be a pattern. I knew that he was going to get in my head again. Violate me. Continue to fuck with me. Take pleasure in the fact that I'm a pawn in some sort of twisted game he's playing. Who is he? Who am I to him?

Was I just the next victim of this man who was not a man at all?

I stormed off to the casino. It was the only thing that was open.

At the casino, all of the machines are dull and lifeless. Except one. It's sparkling and bold. It stood out amongst the rows of its counterparts. The most decorated house in the neighborhood on Christmas eve, festive and bright. Its lights blinked and flashed more intensely than the others. It whirled and beeped louder than the others. It had a glowing halo shining around it. It's the only one making noise now, the only one with flashing lights. All of the other machines have powered down. Now they are gone. They've disappeared. There's only that one machine in the whole room now. It's like it's trying to get my attention. It is trying to get my attention. It's got my attention.

It pulled me towards it and I didn't even notice that no one else was in the casino. It's just me and this machine. The whole casino is white now. And quiet. Silent. There are no walls. No ceiling or floor. There are two things in the entire universe at this moment. There is me and there is this machine.

"THE PENDULUM"

Is the name of it, lit up in blinding multicolored letters. The screen displays an old grandfather clock with a pendulum that sways back and forth against the reels. It's different from the slots I played yesterday, or the day before. The novelty of this particular machine is that the reel spins forwards and backwards, instead of just forward, as was stated on its in-game instructions. I kept reading.

"If the reel spins in reverse, you can change your choices, you can make different decisions. You can turn back time to win! If you don't win the first time, you get a second chance. When the reel spins backwards you can change the outcome. You can change your luck. Change your life."

CHAPTER NINE:
SWALLOW

THUD.

There is noise again. The chattering of people all around me in the casino. So many people. The walls, ceiling and floor are all back. A kaleidoscope of radiant colors. The other machines flashed just as brightly again. Everything is suddenly normal. And then it is not.

Most everyone inside has rushed to an outside deck, especially those closest to the glass doors. Patrons and staff alike, shivering and huddled in the cold. They are investigating the THUD sound. Not all of the people are outside though, there are plenty still stationed at their machines and tables, unmoving, uncaring. Slot zombies.

"Just another Tuesday." A woman chuckles to herself near me.

I approached the outside railing with the others. The THUD sound had broken me from my spell and I was also curious to see what the commotion was.

A man had jumped from his balcony. His balcony that was located on the seventh floor. Even though there were only six floors when I had arrived.

On May 1st 1947, a woman named Evelyn Mchale leapt to her death from the Empire State Building. She landed on a parked car below and it crumpled like a soda can from the force of her fall. But somehow her body remained fully intact upon impact, sprawled out and resting on the now crushed car, in a way that was so natural it appeared graceful, intentional even, like she was laying down and striking a pose for the camera. Which was a bit ironic, as someone had in fact snapped a photo of her.

In the photo, her slender legs stretch out and cross over one another, in the way that dainty women often do, with her toes pointing up to the sky. Her arms at her sides, both hands in driving gloves, which was what classy women wore in the forties, her left hand gently nestled under her chin. No blood appeared anywhere in the photo and if you didn't know any better you might even assume that she was just an old time Hollywood actress on the set of a black and white movie, merely playing dead on top of a prop car in between scenes. She even took the time to do her make up beforehand, as evident by her long lashes and painted lips, which were said to be the shade of a rich garnet red by the witnesses that day. Her eyes were closed, her face untouched by any kind of brutality and her final expression was one of peace.

The photo circulated around the globe and quickly became infamous. It appeared on magazine and newspaper covers and is now known as "The Most Beautiful Suicide."

The man's body below me was the opposite of that.

In the snow, his head was split in half like a big juicy watermelon served on a marble white cutting board. Blood gushed out into a wide crimson pool beneath him. His brain matter was scattered up the sidewalk, chunks of it all over the place, as if you couldn't even believe a head could hold so much brain. The force of impact had caused his eyes to bulge out from their sockets. I think they would have deflated if you poked at them. His tongue hangs out of his mouth like a cartoon character, except there's nothing funny about it. Everything is coated red- his shirt, his pants, his cracked open face, the snow around him. A woman is heard screaming above. A long guttural moan. His wife? I understood her pain, what that wailing meant. I'm probably one of the few in the crowd that does. The pool of blood beneath him grows wider and takes the shape and appearance of what a full wine bottle looks like when spilled, leaving an impossibly large stain of merlot behind. The scene was so gruesome it would make even the most experienced veteran blush.

Security is now surrounding the man's dying body. I can hear the gurgling of his labored gasps, crackling and wet. Some people mistake that for breathing, they get hopeful that their loved one is still alive, that they still have a chance... but it's just saliva rattling in the back of their throat. If anything, it's the opposite- if your loved one is dying and you hear those pained labored gasps, then they're already gone. They call it the "death rattle" for a reason.

Ten minutes ago, his brain was home to around 60 billion neurons. Now it is a ghost town.

Security shined their flashlights onto the gathering crowd. "Okay folks, show's over. Get back to your games." They shouted and we all shuffled back inside. There's a hushed conversation going on among the people standing next to me and I join in with them.

"Jeez, this is the craziest thing that's happened since Jeff was murdered in the lounge." Says one.

"Do you remember when that lady drowned in the pool? When'd that happen? 2019, 2018?" Says another.

"Oh yeah, it must've been 2018 because that's when the Eagles won the Superbowl, I remember I ate good that night."

"You bet on the Eagles?"

"You didn't?"

"Did any of you know this guy?" I asked, since I was just kinda standing there.

"I mean, it's hard to tell, with his face being so fucked up and all, but I don't think so."

"Shit, you don't think that was Mike, do you?" asks another.

"Naw, Mike's in the hospital right now. He had a heart attack the other night after he lost at the horse races again. He didn't look good."

"God damn," I chimed in, "this place seems cursed."

"Yeah, this casino will swallow you up." He responds.

They all nod their heads in agreement.

"Those fucking centipedes man, what was that all about?"

A few people laugh, one shrugs his shoulders.

"I don't even know, got some real weirdos here right now. Some kinda thing going on in the convention hall this week."

"Fuckers got into my suitcase, got in my bed. Shit man, the casino better put some credit in our accounts for having to deal with that bullshit, for real."

They all nod again.

"I used to work pest management," says a man who hadn't spoken yet, "I dealt with all kinds of bugs. With spiders, they tend to warn you if they're about to bite, usually with some kind of threat display. Centipedes will just walk along and bite you out of nowhere... and those big species pack some serious venom. Enough to kill a cat. I would absolutely never hold one... and I will handle a LOT of things."

"Well, shit man. They better put a LOT of credit in our accounts then."

Outside of the crowd, Winter by Vivaldi was playing once again. It sounded as if a lady was humming it quietly to herself. I scanned the room, but couldn't tell who it was. I just knew that song was following me. Someone was following me.

I left the casino floor as the sun was rising. Outside of the tall windows I passed by near the entrance, the morning rays of sunlight reflected off of the blood stained snow, glossy and glistening, still fresh from last night's suicide. Morbid but almost beautiful, in a way. A bold painting to remind us that we are all artists. Unpredictable and mad.

Later that morning, at the cafe, I bumped into my redneck friend. He had already heard about the night's events. News travels fast in this self contained neighborhood, and like with any neighborhood, there's gossip to be had. He told me that he saw the crime scene cleaners outside on his way in this morning. That he could see the vultures circling above as the cleaners did their job.

"Hell of a mess," he said. "The man jumped straight down onto the pavement, so after they removed the body it was just a matter of shoveling the snow up until it wasn't red any more."

"Yeah, I saw the aftermath. I was in the casino when it happened."

I told him.

"You were at the casino that late? You must not have gotten much sleep, you look tired."

"I'm fine" I barked back, surprising myself with the tone of my voice. "No, you're right." I apologized, "I haven't been getting any sleep at all. I've been having strange dreams."

"Oh yeah, you too, huh?" he went on, "I had a real doozy last night. I dreamt I was in a factory or something, some big warehouse. And I was working there, and then a bird flew in, a big brown bird, as big as you or me, and it was flying around tryin' to eat me. It tried to swallow me up. I guess I was a worm or something. It was a weird fucking dream, man."

I hesitated to say anything, not knowing how to respond. Was he one of them? Was this some code or cryptic message The Swindler was trying to send me? A factory dream? What was he trying to tell me?

I stutter, "T-this resort, it's pretty much its own neighborhood, right? Everyone kinda knows everyone else?"

"Yeah, I've been coming here for so long, I've seen a lot of people come and go over the years. I know pretty much everybody." He says warmly.

"What can you tell me about this one guy, he's real tall and has messy brown hair. Wears jewelry. Always has a group of people following him."

"I don't know who you're talking about." Now it's him barking at me, and he quickly changes the subject.

...

I spent the rest of the day by myself, wandering the halls, in and out of the casino. A little time at the bar. Back to the casino. Constantly getting pulled back into the casino. Back to that one specific slot game. The Pendulum. Pulled back in until I was deeper and deeper in the red.

But not talking to anyone else, not knowing who could be a sycophant. Not knowing who I could trust, if anyone, at all. Just keeping to myself. Biding my time.

God's reach is limited. There are no sermons at the poker table. No scripture being read by the cocktail waitresses. If you listen closely, you might hear someone praying for a win, but more often than not, their prayers go unanswered. That's when they wind up on the pavement.

The stars that night were so many and so bright. A galaxy of constellations above the resort, swirling around like glittering white opals in a bowl of black ink. The whole building was beaming with pride. Delighted with the gratification of having swallowed up another victim. The curse that surrounded The Lucky Owl was pleased with its new sacrifice and you could see it in the sky.

I laid in bed, gazing out into the night and wondered, "How many victims has this casino swallowed up? Am I next?"

I have to leave this place. I have to get out of here. I'm not safe. I have to leave this place… as soon… as I break even.

CHAPTER TEN: SACCHARINE

It's the morning before the accident. This afternoon I will lose her. Next week I will watch as they lower her casket into the ground. But this morning, Lauren is alive, laying next to me, breathing into the small of my neck. I turn to kiss her forehead and she wakes up for the last time and in that moment, everything is okay.

She curls up on me and smiles, squeezing my side, wrapping her arms tightly around me. Just one eye barely opened, still groggy and tired but so god damn beautiful.

"Good morning."

It's that time between twilight and dawn. The only noises are the fan quietly humming on the nightstand next to us and a bird chirping, perched in a tree outside of our window, singing its morning song, letting the other birds know that it survived the night. Lauren's warm legs lay on top of mine, the grooves of her body pressed up against me.

She tells me of plans she has that weekend, of seeing all of her buddies to celebrate their friend's pregnancy, a baby shower where everyone will come dressed in pinks or blues. I want to warn her that she will never go to that party. Those same friends will come to her funeral dressed in blacks and grays. But right now she's alive, perfect and whole, and I don't want to ruin it, so I say nothing and just hold her.

"I baked a practice cake yesterday, but I didn't like how it turned out."

"Hmm? Practice cake?"

"Yeah, I didn't tell you? I'm making Heather's gender reveal cake for the party. She's having a girl."

Lauren's face lights up. She knows something that the rest of the party doesn't. She smiles, like a giddy child who peeked through the wrappings of all their siblings' Christmas presents as they slept.

"That's wonderful." *I tell her, and for a brief moment I forget the fate that soon awaits her.*

"They want me to make a German chocolate cake, it's Heather's favorite and she loves mine the most. I have this expensive bright pink food coloring that is supposed to show through anything, even chocolate. But I can't figure it out, the dye won't show up clearly no matter what I do. It just bleeds into the brown cake and turns the whole thing into an ugly muddled red mess. I'd much prefer working with a vanilla base so that the color would really pop but Heather doesn't like vanilla."

Maybe I could change this. Maybe I could turn back time, get a second chance.

"Stay home today. Keep practicing on the cake until you get it right. You don't have to go to work. Just call out. It'll be fine. Focus on making the perfect cake."

I hold her tighter hoping she'll listen.

"No. No, I can't. I won't need a whole day to work on it anyway, I'll get the colors sorted out. I might even use a pink pudding for the middle. Like a cherry flavor. What do you think? It should only take me an *evening to get it right."*

"No, please stay home. You can't go to work today."

I hold her so tight. So close. My legs are now on top of hers, and they wrap around her lower half, resting on top of her. I can smell the remnants of last night's shampoo in her hair.

"Hmm, German chocolate cake wouldn't taste good with cherry flavoring. The flavors wouldn't compliment each other well. Oh! I could make a black forest cake, maybe Heather would compromise on that. I think the party would enjoy it, a black forest cake with pink cherry pudding in the middle. That's it."

She looks at me for approval.

"But German chocolate is your specialty." I try to stall the conversation, but she brushes me off.

The sun is fully in the sky now, it's almost time to get dressed for work. She pulls away from me, gets out of bed and slips off her pajamas.

"Lauren. You have to stay home. Please be with me. Just for today. Please."

"What's wrong? Are you okay?" She's never seen me like this before. I can't hold back any longer.

"Something bad is going to happen at work today."

"What do you mean??"

As she asks me this, she stumbles backwards onto the bed. Confused, she holds onto my arm for balance. She starts to ask more questions, frantic questions, when her body begins to break down.

Her hair falls out in clumps. Her flesh tears away from the bone. She screams and tries to hold her skin tight against her body but there's too much, there's so much skin. Her intestines dangle on the outside of her body, but still attached to her. She's clutching them, they're looped around her hands like eels, and she's trying desperately to shove them back inside.

Now her teeth are falling out, one by one. Then her left eye. She grabs it and pushes it back in, but it slides right back out.

"WHAT IS HAPPENING? What is happening to me?!!" She wails, pleading for answers, for anything.

She's dying. She knows now. I've shattered the illusion.

A broken doll, her legs and arms, fingers and toes, all in pieces. Her bones, sharp and jagged. They poke out of her skin, some crumbling into splinters and fragments.

Our bed is now full of her limbs. A bloody pile of her scattered about on top of the bedsheets. They don't resemble her any more.

It all happened so fast. She just fell apart in front of me.

The less you sleep, the more vivid your dreams are.

I awoke alone on my resort room bed, cold and clammy, shivering like a drowned rat.

Inhale.

One thing to hear: A crowd of people having a conversation in the hallway, right outside of my door.

Two things to touch: The bedsheets that clung to my skin, drenched in cold sweat and spilled liquor. My clothes, also wet, but warm.

Three things to see: The emptiness of the room. The emptiness of the room. The absence of Lauren.

Exhale.

The dream. It felt so real.

CHAPTER ELEVEN: SOLITAIRE

Who were all of these people in the hallway just outside my room? Are they connected to The Swindler? More sycophants? Are they talking about me? What are they saying?

I placed my ear against the door. It's all muffled and I can't make anything out. These people that follow him. He uses them somehow. They follow him and they must have a reason. Or are they following him against their will? What does he want with them? The lady in the elevator, her eyesight was missing. He picked that man's teeth up off the floor. Why? They follow him around like a flock of sheep.

The voice from before speaks inside my head. His voice.

"Well, what's a flock for, if not to fleece?"

The sycophants followed me when I left my room and walked down the hallway. I recognized them all, familiar faces from the bar and lobby. I didn't feel safe anywhere. I could feel their presence on my back. They were stalking me.

How do they know where I am, it seems like they always know where I am.

Oh shit.

The centipede.

Oh God I forgot about the centipede in my ear. Oh God. Oh fuck. How could I forget?

The fucking centipede.

It must be a tracking device.

The convenience store on the lower level was opened now. I snatched up a pair of tweezers and didn't bother paying. In a nearby bathroom, I dug at my ear. I dug so deep down into the canal that I bled trying to reach it. I scraped and scratched and when I finally hit my eardrum I yelped out in pain.

I couldn't grab the fucking thing. It must've crawled its way inside of my brain.

It was too late. The centipede was in too deep.

I was in too deep. I just had to win my money back. I just needed to break even.

I'm going to win my money back and then I'm going to get the fuck out of here for good.

My eyes darted back and forth, frantically scanning everyone I passed as I made my way back to the casino. They whispered into their phones about me. They stared back at me, they all stared back in unison, like every single one of them were all being controlled by the same entity. He wants me next. Ever since we made eye contact in the lobby. He wants to add me to his collection. I could feel, with bone deep certainty, that I was their prey.

They were closing in on me. Stalking behind me. All of them at once. Getting closer, surrounding me. I ducked into a storage room to hide.

The storage room was more like a closet, dark and cramped. The sound of my shallow breathing filled up the small space. The walls were getting tighter but I couldn't go back out there. I had to decide what was worse, my claustrophobia or these stalkers. They had all gathered on the other side of this door, just waiting to devour me.

There was a cellar door under my feet. Beyond the latch were stairs that lead down to a lower level, which I assumed had to have been the basement. I hoped it would take me to somewhere safer.

As I reached the last few steps, I realized that it was not at all what I was expecting. Instead of a dark basement, filled with cleaning supplies or other storage items, I was in an enormous, empty, warehouse-like space. Brightly lit and carpeted. It didn't seem natural, it stretched on forever, longer and wider than the actual resort building itself. But how? So much vast and vacant space. None of this was adding up for me, I couldn't reconcile what I was seeing.

When I turned around to look back for the stairs I came down on, they were nowhere. Gone. Like they were never there and I was always here.

There was perfect silence aside from rows and rows of overhead fluorescent lights, buzzing quietly but at a constant. The closest wall was very far away, but I could make out its peeling, yellowed wallpaper. I started to walk, the green carpet that stretched on forever was worn out everywhere, there was no patch of it that wasn't old and beat up, and it smelled strongly of mildew. It resembled the green felt of a vintage poker table that had been left out in the sun and abandoned for years.

And walked.

I don't know how much time has passed.

After a long while I understood that this place was beyond the measure of time. I knew this because I was never hungry or tired. Never needed water or rest. I got the feeling that it was a concept that wasn't accepted down here.

Before time had meaning, there was no "before." There is no after. There was just this thin veil of space, with nothing to tether me down. I kept walking, trying to find an exit. Trapped in a perpetual state of suspension.

In the absence of time, you start to feel very small. Like a flick of a second on a clock. A pen dot on a globe. Unimportant. A single particle of sand caught in a glass slide under a child's microscope. I was going to die down here.

The warm analogue glow of the lights replaced the sun. Replaced the moon and the stars. My artificial skyline. The scratchy green carpet was now my artificial grass.

The buzzing from the rows of fluorescent lights was always at a constant.

I reached a place where the carpet was different. Still green, but now coarse and shaggy. Even worse, it was all slightly damp- although I didn't see any source of water anywhere. There were rooms far in the distance. They appeared to be empty office rooms. I didn't understand. I couldn't wrap my head around it, couldn't make sense of any of it.

I don't know how many days have passed.

I laid down sometimes, weighted down by anxiousness, uncertainty, then after nothing changed, the unrelenting

76

boredom of absolute nonexistence. The carpet, always damp, felt like a stray dog's mangy fur against my skin. Smelled like it too. I tried so hard to find spots that weren't so rough or musty. I couldn't.

These catacombs that I was going to occupy for all of eternity, had all the charm of a parking garage at 3am with none of the exits. A roach motel without the closure of death. No finality, no epilogue. Wet cement that never dries.

I picked at the carpet. I picked at scabs on my skin that couldn't heal without time. I tried to tear down the peeling wallpaper, but it wouldn't budge, so I pulled at the threads on my shirt. After they had fully unraveled, I pulled out my eyelashes.

Nothing had meaning anymore, tangible or abstract. There was no such thing as objects or ideas. Nothing solid to touch or hold or punch.

I couldn't remember anything. I couldn't make memories because memories exist in time and time didn't exist down here. I couldn't recall what an exit was, or what stairs were, or who I was. I wandered, like a biblical man in the desert, searching for something that was forgotten eons ago.

The buzzing from the rows of fluorescent lights was always at a constant.

I reached the office rooms. Each one was the same as the last. Room after room, all bare and tinted pale green, with only short hallways between them. I walked through dozens of rooms with nothing in them but the buzzing of the overhead fluorescent lights above.

There was one room. There was a room with a hole in it and a large gray rock next to the hole.

I picked up the rock and held it. A solid thing in my hands. I indulged in its smooth sides. I welcomed the edges and crevices.

Took gratitude in its dark gray color after only experiencing nothing but wave after wave of yellow and green.

After the admiration had worn off, I dropped it in the hole. The first new thing I had done in weeks. Months? I waited to hear the rock hit the bottom, but the sound never came.

I walked through several more rooms, hoping to find something novel once more in one of them. The hole was miles behind me now, but I never found anything like it again.

The average person doesn't take into account the significance that isolation can have on your mental health. They say that we've abolished cruel and unusual punishment, but ask any prisoner that has spent time in solitary, and they will tell you otherwise.

The buzzing from the rows of fluorescent lights was always at a constant.

How was I still alive?

For the first time, the lights began to flicker. Then shut off. My artificial sun had powered down.

Now there was nothing but darkness, space and the absence of time.

Until I heard the rumbling of machinery below.

It churned and cranked. It muffled the sounds of Lauren screaming. I had to find her. I remember who I am. Things come rushing back. Thoughts, memories. Fears.

It's pitch black. I could only hear Lauren screaming. I tried to find her, I followed her screams. I reached for her in the darkness, to bring her back to me. My arms were in front of me, but I couldn't see them. They were just reaching out, reaching for a desperate attempt at hope. At clutching something, anything. A disembodied scream.

The lights came back on. It's quiet again.

Lauren wasn't here but I'm not alone, there was something nearby. A bad presence. Its eyes watched me in the distance.

Someone had been following me this whole time.

"There is a sound that only the dying can hear. Can you hear it yet, Russell?"

I turn around and see him. The Swindler. He is in one of the many rooms behind me. When he sees that I've spotted him, he sinks into the wall and disappears.

But The Swindler wasn't by himself. There was another man. A maintenance man with a vacuum. He is vacuuming the carpet. The catacombs are now one room. One small room and nothing more.

The endless rows of fluorescent lights are gone and only one dim light bulb hangs above our heads. There are cleaning supplies everywhere, there are shelves and tables and tools. They fill the space of the small storage room that I was suddenly occupying.

I try to focus on the maintenance man, my eyes adjusting to the light, to this new reality I've shifted into. He had badly burnt skin, red and warped and scaly. I was taken aback and recoiled.

"Did he do this to you? Did he take your skin?"

"What the Hell? Get the fuck out of here! You're not supposed to be in here." He scolded me harshly, like an angry father about to beat his son.

He pointed to a door on the wall that had always been right there, eight feet to the left of me.

"If you don't leave right now, I'm calling security." He pointed to the exit again before reaching for his walkie talkie that was strapped to his utility belt.

"No, you don't have to do that. I'm leaving."

When I walked through the door, It opened into the middle of the casino. Right in front of The Pendulum slot machine in all of its glory, waiting for me to play.

Chess takes skill. Even checkers and tic-tac-toe take skill. Slots are just luck, you're just going through the motions and hoping for the best. There's an analogy in there somewhere, but it's lost on me.

It's not even really a game, there was no strategy to learn- you don't grow or become better at it. It's not enriching or thought provoking or fun even. You just keep pulling. And pulling. And pulling. So why was it so addicting? Why does it light up all the dopamine centers in my brain? Why couldn't I pull myself away from it?

The animated sprite behind the screen lights up- it was a blonde woman, made of code and pixels. She spouted off her catchphrases to me in a computerized voice, with a smile on her face but nothing behind her digital eyes.

"Keep spinning!" "Let's turn back time!" "Are you sure you want to stop playing?" "Come back! Keep playing- here's a bonus game!" "Your hot streak meter is almost full!"

Every time I was low on money, a bonus game or a secret level would pop up, enticing me to pull the lever again. Reeling me back in. Feeding me just enough money back into my account so that I could continue playing. Hypnotized by this reel that spun forwards and backwards and handed out second chances like candy.

The Swindler was always close by. At poker tables or roulette wheels. Slithering like a hog-nosed snake between aisles of slot machines, made up in equal parts of serpent and swine. Slipping in and out of these four casino walls that confined us. Sneaking behind me. Watching me play. And his sycophants were so close, so close that I felt their warm breath on the back of my neck. Then I heard them whisper a message to me.

"Don't think he won't skin you when your skin is all that is left."

"Be sober-minded; be watchful. Your adversary the devil prowls around like a roaring lion, seeking someone to devour." 1 Peter 5:8

CHAPTER TWELVE: STILLBORN

"Don't get too close to me today, I must've caught a cold or some kinda virus. I'm all stuffed up, can't smell nothin' since yesterday." The redneck tells me when I walked through the door to the cafe.

He seemed to live here, at this cafe. He was my only friend here, even if I couldn't trust him. A semblance of a friend. My one connection to humanity.

There were children running around, unattended. Little children, no older than six or seven. Jumping on chairs, stacking containers of creamer and packets of sugar high up on tabletops, pulling books off the shelves, hiding behind tall plants.

"Are these your grandkids?" I asked him.

"No, not mine. I mean, they might as well be, I've watched them grow up here. A lot of parents just leave their kids upstairs all day while they play the slots. No kids allowed downstairs in the casino area. I've seen the same kids runnin' around since they were in diapers, it's pretty sad if I think about it. I guess I just don't really think about it too much."

He continues,

"Ya know, every addict is someone's family member. Those kids could be home for the holidays right now instead of this. I know it, I'm one of them. I've seen parents miss their kids' school plays, graduations. Hell, I missed my own son's baseball games when he was little, now he doesn't even speak to me. But at least I never forgot about him, at least I kept him alive."

"What do you mean?" I asked.

"I wasn't here for it, I was in Philadelphia for work at the time, but a manager who I'm buddies with told me that this lady used to come in to play the slots every day. Turns out she had a baby, like a little baby, right? And she'd leave her in the car under the shade in the parking lot and go check on her every so often. So one morning, she's on a winning streak, right? She's racking up winnings back to back and she completely loses track of time. Hours pass and the sun is in a completely different place in the sky. There ain't no shade no more. Someone came across her car that evening with the baby still inside. It was too late. Baby's dead. The cops came and took the lady away, nobody ever saw her again."

"Fuck." I said, while the unattended children ran in circles around us.

The beautiful woman from the bar walks in, the same escort who was trying to fuck me a few days ago. Turns out it's her kids. She calls out for them and they come running. She's haggard looking, worn down, I hardly recognise her. She smells of sour body odor covered in coconut lotion, like she's trying to hide it. The tropical scent doesn't mask the stink though, it just adds to it. It permeates against the aroma of rich coffee and sweet pastries, causing everything in the cafe to smell like expired milk.

Her hair is greasy, slicked flat to her scalp. She's wearing the same clothes that I saw her in last. Her white sweater is now dingy, lightly stained at the pits and stretched out. The collar of her sweater droops down her shoulder revealing an old bra strap. The big diamond bracelet she was wearing was nowhere to be found.

"Jesus Christ, Farrah, you look like shit." The redneck says.

"Same to you, Bill." She looks him up and down, then gathers her kids up and leaves.

"It's never enough, is it?" He says to me but also to the room in general. He's waxing poetic in his own way. "This is a desperate place filled with desperate people."

"Must be rough with her trying to work with her kids around. That's a real shit lifestyle that she's exposing them to."

"What do you mean?"

"She's an escort, isn't she?"

"Nah, Farrahs not a hooker. What makes you say that?"

"Oh. I just thought... nevermind."

"She's just in here with the rest of us. Her only vice is gambling, I mean, as far as I know."

There's a silence between us now. It's not an uncomfortable one, but it lingers for a bit. I take a sip of my coffee and we both just kind of stare off past each other, our eyes fixated on nothing.

Anyways, I saw something movin' around in my room last night," he breaks the silence and continues, "it must have been one of those centipedes."

He then started scratching at his leg and he didn't stop, even after a weirdly long time. And now the silence is uncomfortable. I watched him, not knowing what else to do or how exactly to react.

Scratch

Scratch

Scratch

Scratch

Scratch

"Are you okay?" I finally asked.

"Yeah. God, it's just so itchy. The damn thing must've bit me or something. It itches real bad."

...

That night, for the first time since Laurens death, I didn't dream about her. I dreamt about that little baby, trapped in the hot car.

I'm standing in the parking lot and I know the baby is still alive. It's summer now and even in just a t-shirt and shorts I can feel the beads of sweat collecting on my forehead, down my neck and under my arms. I spot her mother's car and run to her, to rescue her, this chubby little infant. but as I run, the car keeps moving further away. The asphalt is like sticky black taffy, stretching, getting longer and longer and now there is so much time and distance between the baby and I that I start to panic.

Although I'm miles away, I can somehow see the baby. Such is the nature of dreams. As of now, she is okay, cooing and smiling, her fingers in her little toothless mouth. She bobs her head left and right and giggles at the leaves on the trees that she can see from outside of the backseat window. I can see the baby but I just can't get to her. I run but the car keeps moving further and further away. She's always just out of reach.

The sun rises far into the sky and the cars are no longer under the tree's shade in the parking lot. It's high noon now and the blazing heat bears down, punishing the baby for the crime of being born to a neglectful mother.

It's sweltering. It's so fucking hot that it must be the middle of July, the dog days of summer. The sweat drips down my face. The parking lot asphalt sizzles.

The baby is now clearly in distress and she starts to pull at the short blonde tufts of her hair. She thrashes and claws at the seatbelt and then at her face. Her skin turns a pinkish red and begins to rise and blister as the car quickly becomes a makeshift oven. She's been screaming in pain for close to an hour at this point, her tiny voice is so hoarse, so raspy and strained.

She's spitting up formula and convulsing now, covered in warm vomit. Crying out for her mother who is not there, because she is too busy pulling the lever on the Sexy Babes of Miami slot machine. The baby's skin is now at a boiling point, it sloughs off of her in small peeling clumps. Her body's temperature continues to rise until it is so high that it becomes incompatible with life. The tiny blood vessels in her eyes burst and finally, she stops crying.

That's when I'm allowed to reach her. And of course it's too late.

I picked her up and cradled her, this poor dead baby in my arms. We're all alone in the parking lot, standing next to her mothers car. I held her close to my chest and apologized to her. Her fate was already etched in stone. It was inevitable, and I was just a visitor. An observer of this cruel outcome that had already transpired months ago. I rocked her gently and sang her a quiet lullaby. There was nothing else I could do.

And then the vultures came.

I was surrounded by the darkness of my room. My heart, beating inside my throat. I could only hear a grinding scraping sound.

Nothing to smell, nothing to see, one thing to hear.

It was the gnashing of my own teeth.

CHAPTER THIRTEEN: SONGBIRD

Two years ago, Lauren and I had a conversation in our bedroom. The conversation that is now a permanent echo in my head. In another timeline, maybe it would've gone differently and she would be here with me today. How each seemingly small choice shapes us all so profoundly. Each time I think back to the conversation, I die with her all over again. A feedback loop of suffering on repeat, as real as any physical wounds that can make a man fall to his knees and succumb to death.

There's a reason some spouses pass on soon after their partner does, they "die of a broken heart." I used to think that saying was melodramatic and not actually possible, but the anguish that I feel is so tangible that it has become solid and could very well kill me. It's this solid object that has transcended my mental state and crossed over into the material world. And it's plunged deep into me, heavy and sharp. A knife.

No matter how hard I try, I can't pull it out. The knife is solid, but it's shaped like a song. A loud jagged melody that twists its way through me and doesn't stop, it never stops. It only gets louder.

I'm still in my resort room, laying in bed after waking up from another nightmare. I'm just passing the time with my own personal footage of hell that plays in my head every time I'm alone with my thoughts.

It's one year before the accident.

We're sitting on our bed together. Lauren has just gotten home from work and she's exhausted. Another shit day at her job. She's had enough.

"I thought making it to management would change things." She laments. "I thought it would be better. But she's still such a bitch to me. I don't even know what I did to her for her to hate me so much. I think she's just like that. How can somebody just be like that? She's not even my superior anymore. You know, we just had the most stressful fucking Black Friday ever and I'm just so over it. She plays this cheesy Christmas music, the same CD all day. It's nothing but Jingle Bells, Last Christmas and Santa Baby, for eight long hours. Every fucking day. For two months straight. It's torture. You know I love Christmas time babe, but I want to dash my God damn head on a one horse open sleigh."

"Aww baby, don't do that. I can't have you dashing your head on anything. You know, all I want for Christmas is you." I sing to her in the worst Mariah Carey impression anyone has ever done ever.

And she rightfully smacks me with her pillow.

"So I finally snapped today, I couldn't take it anymore. I went back to the office, ripped that fucking CD out of the player and snapped it in half. And this bitch. Do you know what she did? This icy, miserable bitch looked at me, reached into her desk drawer without even breaking eye contact, and pulled out a second copy of the same exact CD. I have to quit, I can't work there another day."

I let her continue to vent.

"It's just soul crushing. Anything would be better. I could get a job at the airport, maybe go back to waitressing. Oh! I think the library is hiring, I could be a librarian. That would be pretty cool."

"What about baking full time? You could turn it into a career."

"I don't know, it's such a fun hobby for me. I'm afraid if I turn it into a full time thing it won't be fun anymore, it'll be work."

"How about joining me at the factory?"

"What? Are you for real? Won't I need a lot of training? It has got to be all men there, right? I'm not strong enough."

"No! You'd be surprised, there's a few women there. It's not all heavy lifting. It's not hard either, they'll have you trained in a few days, tops."

"I don't know. I'm so old. I think I'd rather be a friendly old librarian lady. I could wave my finger at the rambunctious youth and shout "Shh! No talking" anytime they make a ruckus." She jitters her pointer finger like an elderly librarian and we laugh.

"Old? What are you talking about? You're only thirty four! C'mon babe, it'll be great! The money is good, we can drive up together and you'll pick up the basics in no time."

She hesitates at first, letting the idea slosh around back and forth in her head for a bit.

"I mean, spending more time with you is definitely a positive. Plus, I guess we'll save on gas money. Oh! And we can have lunch breaks together! We can complain about coworkers! We can sneak around and grope each other when no one is looking. Okay, okay, I'm in."

I reach behind me and reveal a box that I've hidden under our bed.

"Surprise! I got you an early Christmas gift, well, consider it a celebration present."

She squeals and quickly unwraps it, creating shreds of wrapping paper around her.

"Here's to better days at work, spending more time with each other and never having to deal with that awful bitch again. To happier times."

It's a jewelry box. Painted light blue and adorned with tiny metallic snowflakes that gleam when the light hits them.

"I saw you eyeing up that exact one when we went to the mall last month. Is that the one you wanted?"

"Yes! This is the one! I love it, it's perfect! Thank you."

When she opens up the top of the lid, a plastic ballerina twirls around on her pointed toe, and a classical song plays. It's a song that I'm very familiar with. It's a song I know quite well.

And now that song is a knife, a sharp melody that continues to cut deep into me every time I think about her. And all of my thoughts lead back to her.

KNOCK KNOCK KNOCK

"Room service!" The voice shouts from the other side of my door. The knock is so loud, I jump from being startled out of my daydream. I cracked open the door slightly, and peered through, leaving the chained lock on. You can never be too careful, especially here.

"Hello, room service," he says again, "I've brought up your order."

"I didn't order room service."

"Are you sure?" The bellhop looks down at the receipt in his hand, then up at the room number, then back to me. "Is your name Russell Clark?"

"Yes, but I didn't order room service."

"Well, this receipt says otherwise. Here you are." He hands me a small styrofoam container through the door and then leaves.

Inside the container was a single slice of black forest chocolate cake, with pink pudding in the middle.

I don't eat it.

CHAPTER FOURTEEN: STALEMATE

Cards are war in disguise as a sport- Charles Lamb

I'm back at the casino, in front of The Pendulum. I'm pulling the lever but acutely aware of my surroundings. One eye on the reel and one eye on the room. There's a bachelor party to the right of me, visibly wasted and overly friendly to anyone within earshot. They're hooting and hollering in celebration, "Kevin is getting married! Our bro is getting hitched, yeah son! Our fucking boy!" The party tells me that they've hired strippers for their room and they ask me to join them, to share a drink and a hooker in honor of their groom-to-be. There is nothing in the world I want more than to not be a part of that, so I politely decline.

Nearby, I spot him. The Swindler is at the roulette table. He's in my line of sight.

He bets everything on black and the roulette wheel spins round and round, until it slows down and lands on black.

He bets all of his winnings on black, and the wheel stops on black again.

He bets his growing pile of winnings on black, and again, the wheel does as it is told.

He bets his mountain of winnings on red, the wheel stops on red and I find myself at a red table, sitting on a red chair, with him on the opposite side. All around us it's pitch black, save for the whites of his followers eyes as they watch us.

"We got off on the wrong foot," he tells me. This time, his mouth moves. He finally speaks to me with words out loud.

"Let's play a game of poker. High stakes, of course. It's the only way to play."

He shuffles a deck.

This is the closest I've ever been to him. I can see the details in his face; the lines in his forehead, the depth of his eyes. He looks human enough, but even some tumors have hair and teeth.

"Let's make a deal, Russell. Your body, everyone's bodies, is a box with an expiration date. This box stores the brain, a pulsating slab of meat that cannot comprehend anything but permanence. Together, they create a shivering, thinking, feeling human being. Full of uncertainty. Knowing it will die but not knowing what death is. And so we suffer. We suffer because everything is temporary and futile. We can't pause or rewind or stop death. But what if we could? I can. And I can do that for you."

"How?"

"Time is a thief, but so am I."

"You can travel through time? Can you raise the dead?" When I ask him this question, I'm not skeptical. I'm awe-struck.

The Swindler stops. There is no noise around us. The absence of sound is palpable, almost solid. It's an awkward lump in my throat that I can't swallow. He speaks again.

"Yes, I can bring her back if you win. The Lucky Owl transcends the boundaries of time and space."

"Yeah, I've gathered that. So, are you in control, or does the building have control over you?"

"The building has the power, but over time I've learned to control it." He says all of this so casually, "I can manipulate it to my will. I'm not bound by any laws of reality." He pauses briefly, "I just need one thing from you if you lose."

"And what is that?"

"I need your hearing. It sounds bizarre, I know, but it's how I'm able to continue to thrive. How I'm able to stay on this mortal plane. I gather people's senses and in exchange they can live through me. They feel through me, function through me. And you will too. You'll stay here. No more suffering. I have the abilities of a hundred men. But I always want more."

He pauses.

"It's never enough, is it?" He says to me with the voice of the cafe redneck.

"So I need you, but you have to make a deal with me, and it has to be agreed upon. If you win, you get Lauren back. If I win, I get your hearing."

Sound is such an intimate thing. To never hear another voice again. The sound of a bird's song. A favorite album. An old recording of Lauren and I.

But I had to try.

"Okay, deal."

He deals me a hand. I have one pair. He has a full house.

"You just told me that you have the abilities of a hundred men. How can I win against you?" I question him.

"What other choice do you have? What opportunity will arise where you have this chance to bring her back?" He replies.

"Why my hearing?"

"Hearing is the last sense you lose before you die, Russell, and you're almost dead. You're so close to death. I followed you in the catacombs, I followed you through every room. I watched you unravel and go mad. All of the wrinkles in your brain have corroded with rust. All those years spent in solitude, a hundred lifetimes spent alone. You've managed to make your way out of the catacombs, but you've come back haunted."

He deals me a hand. I have a high card, he has four of a kind.

I watched his fingers closely. There was no trickery, no sleight of hand. He had no loose sleeves to tuck cards away or hidden pockets in his shirt. But I knew this was all a ruse. How can I win a game that was rigged from the start?

He deals again. He has a royal flush. I have nothing.

"I'm done, I'm not playing any longer. I quit."

"You can't do that. Nobody has ever done that before," he calmly states.

I pushed the table away from me and refused to continue playing.

When I stood up to walk away, I instead found myself back at The Pendulum slot machine. I don't know if it was real or if I had zoned out while watching the reel spin and imagined the whole thing.

Truth is, I'm not certain of anything anymore. Actually, I'm certain of one thing. I need to hear Lauren's voice again. There are voicemails of her on my phone.

YOU HAVE 28 MISSED CALLS.
YOU HAVE 15 NEW VOICE MESSAGES.
NEW TEXTS (14)
NEW EMAILS (16)

NEW MESSAGE: "Hey Russ, how are you doing? I completely understand if you'd like to bow out this year, but Dave and I wanted to know if you'll still be over for Christmas. We'd love for you to be here with us. Jen and Brian are here now, they say hi. Call me when you're up to it, take care."

NEW MESSAGE: "Mom wants you to call her, she told me she's called you like twenty times and you're not answering. Please just talk to her."

NEW MESSAGE: "Hey Russell, it's Beth. I am so sorry for your loss. Stacey just told me. If you need anything or just want to talk, give me a call. I know it's been a while but I'm here if you need me."

NEW MESSAGE: "Russell, where are you? We're starting to get worried. Please answer your phone."

NEW MESSAGE: "Hey man, we miss you at work. Check in with us sometime soon and we'll figure something out about relocating you to another site. Let me know if I can do anything to help."

NEW MESSAGE: "Fucking answer your phone, this is serious, mom and dad are really scared. Please. All you have to do is call and just let us know you're okay."

NEW MESSAGE: "HELLO, THIS IS YOUR SHOP-MART PHARMACY. WE ARE CALLING TO LET YOU KNOW THAT YOU HAVE (1) PRESCRIPTIONS TO PICK UP. THANK YOU."

NEW MESSAGE: "Russell honey, if we don't hear back from you, I'm going to have to file a missing persons report. Please call me."

NEW MESSAGE: "Hi, This is Officer Weber. I've been trying to get in touch with you by email. You need to come down to the station and review some things regarding your wife's death."

NEW MESSAGE: "HELLO, THIS IS YOUR SHOP-MART PHARMACY. WE ARE CALLING TO LET YOU KNOW THAT YOU HAVE (3) PRESCRIPTIONS TO PICK UP. THANK YOU"

NEW MESSAGE: "Hey Russ, it's Pete. The mailman knocked on my door just now, says your mailbox is full. He said they're gonna have to hold your mail until you come back, he wanted me to call you to let you know."

NEW MESSAGE: "Just checking in with you, wondering where you are. Rick told me that the supervisor is fixin' to move you over to the Greensburg location. Call me when you get this."

NEW MESSAGE: "I filed a missing persons report. I had to, I don't know what else to do. So, they're looking for you now. Please call me. God, please just call me."

NEW MESSAGE: "THIS IS YOUR SHOP-MART PHARMACY. WE ARE CALLING TO LET YOU KNOW THAT YOU HAVE (4)

PRESCRIPTIONS TO PICK UP. THANK YOU."

NEW MESSAGE: "I've read that when an autopsy is done, they don't put the organs back where they belong. They are all stored in the belly, all together in a big plastic bag, like the giblets of a Thanksgiving turkey.

That poor baby, the one that died in the hot car, her bag must've been so small. Like a tiny ziplock pouch packed inside a kindergartener's lunch box.

And your dear wife, why, there was nothing to bag up, was there Russell? They hosed the floor down and mopped up her remains. What did you mourn at her funeral? Did they just wring the mop out and send you the dirty water in a bucket?"

All of Laurens voicemails are gone. They've been deleted.

CHAPTER FIFTEEN: SACRAMENT

"As the dog returns to his vomit, so does the fool return to his folly."
Proverbs 26:11

What a gambling addict craves is not so much the win, but the rush they feel before knowing the outcome. When the ball is about to land in the roulette, when the horses are in the final meters of the race, when the dealer is about to show the card that can win or lose the game. What that means is that a gambling addict will never be satisfied by winning or getting rich. In the end it is not about the money itself, the prizes or even the jackpot. It is about the adrenaline rush they feel when they experience the anticipation of an unknown outcome.

A while ago, I read about a scientist who was conducting a study where he would drown rats, and he noted that they typically drowned in a few minutes. He then took a few out of the water before they drowned, dried them off, fed them and let them rest.

Then he put them back in the water.

With this newfound sense of hope, these rats endured for hours longer than the control rats, because they had the expectation that they could survive it. The other rats, realizing the hopelessness of their situation, simply gave up and drowned despite being physically capable of surviving much longer. Without hope, the only thing left for life is to succumb to death.

A drunken businessman is on a machine to the left of me. The bachelor party is still to my right.

The businessman is so inebriated that he's slurring his speech. He keeps grabbing my shoulder to steady himself, while his bad breath repeatedly smacks me in the face.

He tells me that he has embezzled money from his company, and that he's been at it for some time. First he dipped into his own funds, then his mortgage and savings. When his wife found out he was embezzling from his company, she left him.

"No no, I'll be honest with you, I'll be honest," He slurred. "It's not a company, not a company, no. It's my church. It's my church and I'm the deacon." He stifles a laugh.

He took my stunned silence as a chance to explain in more detail about the embezzlement and what it all entailed. From what I could gather in his intoxicated rambling, in the beginning he skimmed money from the collection plates, then moved on to taking larger sums from charities the church donated to, and finally, he got really bold and was now using the church's bank card to hit up the ATM directly inside the casino.

Except as he went on, it didn't feel like much of an explanation. It felt like a confession. So much so that he's forced me into this role as his priest, and I'm listening to him confess his sins to me. I was not supposed to know this information. This is forbidden knowledge. Can a deacon even confess to a priest? There should be a latticed wall between us and a curtain covering up our conversation, a private confession that the whole casino is currently bearing witness to.

This drunken man of God contradicts so heavily against the bachelor party next to us.

Next to me are buddies just wanting to have a good time, win some money and hype up their friend. On the other side of me is a desperate criminal, too wayward to keep his secrets to himself, risking jail time and banishment from his community for that adrenaline rush.

Everyone starts off as the former. We're all just looking for a good time. Nobody becomes an addict overnight.

In dog training, when the trainer rewards the dog for doing the right command its dopamine goes up. But if he only rewards it sometimes and unpredictably at that, the dog's dopamine goes through the roof. And it's not the reward that triggers the dopamine. It's the signal to do the command. The chance that a reward may come is the addicting part. It works the same way on rats and on monkeys. And on people.

And it's insidious. Usually gambling addiction first hooks you when you're young and impressionable. A carnival game, a trip to the arcade, a blind box toy with a fun surprise inside.

Religion hooks you when you're young too. No 30 year old is going to believe the stories in the bible if they've never been exposed to them before. This false hope hooks you when you're impressionable, when you're just a kid.

Put your money in the slots or put your money in the collection plate. Each time you'll pray for the hope that you'll attain something bigger than life. And the anticipation of it all, whether it's hitting the jackpot or getting to heaven is more exciting than actually reaching it, because "it" doesn't really exist, does it?

We bet that there's an afterlife and we bet that we deserve to be there, in paradise, amongst the angels and clouds. That life has meaning, that there is something bigger than us. the ultimate jackpot. The prize of heaven, of salvation. And then, as you're praying one night, you get a phone call and find out that your cherished deacon is stealing your tithing money directly from the collection plate.

We're all just gambling men, even when the odds are staring us in the face. There's a fine line between entertainment and exploitation and both the church and the casino industry have figured it out. They've cracked the code. They've perfected the art of predation through false hope.

"Keep spinning!" "Let's turn back time!" "Are you sure you want to stop playing?" "Come back! Keep playing- here's a bonus game!" "Try to unlock the scatter feature!"

The little blonde sprite smiles and dances around on the screen, a pixelated temptress whose only purpose is to keep you playing, long after it stops being fun.

The casino will exploit a spender. The church will exploit a sinner.

But we're not at church. We're not in a confessional booth.

We're in a skinner box.

"It'sa, it's an addiction only if ya lose," the drunk deacon presses his pointer finger into my nose and exclaims, "If you, if you don't lose, it's not an addiction; it's a talent! And I'm a very 'hiccup' talented man."

Give a rat a lever that always dispenses food and he'll just use it when he's hungry. Give a rat a lever that only randomly sometimes dispenses food and he'll sit there and pull it all day.

Until the scientist decides to drown him.

CHAPTER SIXTEEN: SURGEON

Tonight, the view out of my window is thick with dense rolling fog. It's so heavy that it blocks out all of the stars in the night sky. No moonlight, no twinkling white gemstones or swirling constellations that beam with pride. Everything is muted tonight. Everything is dull and gray and lifeless.

Before drifting off to sleep, I hear a loud rumbling sound. But it doesn't sound like the rumbling of machines. It sounds like the rumble of an empty stomach.

I'm inside an immaculate white room. Sterile. Cold. It is a hospital room. An operating room, to be specific. Everything is so neat and orderly, so very clean- the walls, the floor, the operating table. It's a stark contrast to the dizzying, clashing patterns of the casino walls and floor. Everything is so spotless and pristine. Everything except for what is on the operating table.

Lauren's remains lay on the table, a heaping pile of bloody limbs and jagged bones. The same pile that had fallen apart on our bed in my previous dream. The Swindler is wearing doctor's scrubs, he's donned head to toe in faded teal. His name tag reads "Dollmaker" and he's staring into my eyes, unblinking.

There is a metal table next to him. On it are various surgical instruments, amongst them are a scalpel, forceps, scissors, a suture needle and thread.

He picks up the suture needle, which is already attached to a length of nylon thread, then picks up Lauren's severed arm from the pile, and forcefully inserts the needle into the edge of it, piercing the flesh until the needle is all of the way through. He grabs another body part, a piece of her leg maybe? And begins to sew the two parts together.

"I can fix her up, good as new. Don't worry, everything will be okay. I'll fix her right up."

The needle glints in the bright light of the operating room as he works on her.

He keeps a steady hand and a focused expression, moving quickly but precisely.

"In and out, in and out," he says calmly under his breath.

It's a simple interrupted stitch, and he ties each knot tightly to ensure this new body part he has Frankenstein'ed together is properly closed.

Then he sews another piece onto it, another limb, and then another. A big toe sewn on an elbow, a ring finger sewn to her belly. Her face scattered about, a nose here, an eyeball there.

"Almost there."

Each time he attaches another organ or appendage, he reassures me that everything will be okay, all while he continues to desecrate her body. She's now this grotesque lump of mangled body parts, all haphazardly stitched together, resembling nothing.

Her splintered bones poke through parts of her flesh, sticking out in a few places, sharp and jagged.

"There's not enough flesh. Too many bones but not enough flesh," he tells me.

"I'll have to take her bones and wrap new flesh around them."

His face is intense with concentration, his brows are furled and eyes are focused. He's an artist and this is his Mona Lisa. He grabs the scalpel and slices deep into her mutilated skin, creating a fresh gaping wound. Then he reaches down into his pocket and pulls out a large fistful of centipedes. He shoves them inside of the newly opened cavity, putting life back into her.

"There. That should make her wiggle again."

She starts to squirm and writhe, pulsating with lively centipedes that are all riled up and agitated.

Her body parts are all wrong, in all of the wrong places. She's all patched up and moving, but it's not her.

"Please, stop this. Please. Jesus Christ please stop this." I plead to The Swindler, even though I know it's pointless.

He gives her a quick peck on where her forehead should be and holds her tightly.

"Isn't this what you wanted, Russell? She looks much better than before. Healthy, even. Did you get the message I left you? I was just curious about what you actually mourned at her funeral. What did the morgue send you to put in her casket?"

He stuck a piece of gum in his mouth, chewed it up and blew a bubble. When the bubble popped, it jolted me awake.

It's daytime now, but the fog remains thick, opaque in the cold morning air. There's no sunlight that shines through the window when I open my eyes. It's dark, darker than it has ever been. The whole resort is surrounded with this foreboding aura, this bad presence. Even in my room, the fog seems like it has broken through the building and now permeates inside, heavy and gray. I smell nothing. I hear nothing. I see something.

I reach over to turn on the lamp, and that's when I see it.

There's a mop and a bucket, that's full of blood, in the bed with me. I'm not dreaming anymore, this is really happening. I recoiled and jumped back, and when I did, it caused the bucket to tip and spill over. The blood was everywhere now, seeping into the mattress, growing wider, quickly spreading. A whole gallon of blood soaked deep into the bed, spilling over the sides of the bed frame, dripping in a heavy red stream onto the white carpet below. Filling the entire room with the pungent smell of copper.

ENOUGH. Enough. Fucking enough already.

I took off out the door and ran. As if I could outrun it. I ran down the hall, straight to the lobby and noticed something right away.

There is something wrong with the resort. There is something very wrong.

CHAPTER SEVENTEEN: SUBMERGE

"You have put me in the lowest pit, in the darkest depths. Your wrath lies heavily on me; you have overwhelmed me with all your waves. You have taken from me." Psalm 88:6-8

The resort is not pleased, it's not glowing with neon lights anymore. There's no vivid colors in the hallway, no clashing patterns swirling around on the carpet. The slot machines have powered down in the casino. There's no warm pastries or coffee being served in the cafe. It is void of people, completely empty. Vacant. Abandoned. Everything is muted. Faded like an old newspaper photo of a sickly dying man. A weathered obituary that's been tucked away in a cold, dark basement, forgotten by the passage of time.

There have been no new sacrifices in days, no deaths or debts for it to feed on. There's that faint rumbling sound again that penetrates below the building, like an empty stomach aching for something to fill it. It's hungry. The resort is hungry.

The plants that fill its floors are withering, they're shriveled and thin. The leaves droop and are browning at the edges. The deer head mounted in the lobby is wasting away. Its cheeks are sunken in, its fur is falling out leaving patches of exposed dried skin behind, and its mouth is open and filled with clusters of warts.

All of the hallways are skinnier this morning, so skinny you can barely squeeze two people through at a time. The whole building is noticeably smaller. Weaker. The walls are brittle like eggshells, splitting and cracking under the slightest touch. The foundation rattles like a dancing skeleton, and the remnants of an ivory chandelier that had crashed down are now scattered across the floor. The resort is malnourished. Skin and bones. It must be starving.

The Swindler is in the lobby. He's the only other person here. And it's because he is not a person, he's not a person at all.

I've had enough. It's time for me to confront him.

"I know you're following me."

"Huh?" He seemed taken aback.

"I don't want to play your fucked up games anymore."

"What the fuck are you talking about?" His eyes get bigger.

"This is going to stop, you are going to leave me the fuck alone."

"I don't even know who you are, man."

"Fuck you! Don't play stupid with me. I know who you are, I know what you are." I get closer to him, pointing at him, stomping my way towards him.

"Dude, seriously, back up off of me."

"I saw you pick up the teeth!"

"Teeth? What teeth?? Oh, oh man, that was days ago, I was drunk and thought they were pearls or something rolling towards me."

"Why did you release the centipedes?"

"RELEASE? Are you fucking kidding me?? They escaped. I'm here for the convention, it's happening upstairs in the conference hall. I swear to God. I have a booth there. Someone accidentally knocked their tank over and they fucking scattered everywhere man, I couldn't get them all."

He starts to back up, turns and paces away from me, faster and faster.

"No!" I race up to him, keeping up with his pace. "What about the woman whose sight you stole? And the conversation we had the other day where you spoke to me with your mind."

I take a few swings at him, but he dodges them and I don't make contact.

He paces faster now, he's rushing through the lobby and I'm right behind him, chasing him.

"I know what you're up to!" I scream at him, "I know you're controlling everyone here! Taking their eyes and their skin and teeth, taking their sanity! Taking! Taking! Taking! You're a swindler! You're not taking ANYTHING from me!"

He's now running away from me. It's all an act. He's a good actor, he looks absolutely terrified. He has everyone else fooled.

"Oh my God, you're crazy, you're fucking crazy. Get away from me!"

I corner him against a wall, near the gift shop. He has nowhere to run now. I know he could sink into the wall and escape if he really wanted to. I know what I saw. He's got everyone else fooled. Foolish, foolish. Not me. No. He's such a good actor. I can see what's going on. He'll wait until my guard is down and attack. But for now, I have the upper hand.

In the gift shop, there is a box cutter at the register. Its blade is as sharp as any knife. I grab it and I'm ready for this to be over with.

When a person is gravely injured they all get the same look in their eyes, that unmistakable look of fear. It doesn't matter what language they speak, what ethnicity they are, or what God they pray to, when you see that look you immediately understand what is happening to them. A wild animal, void of the natural fear of death, is hard to stop. That's what makes them so dangerous. You have to hurt the animal if you want it to back off and comprehend its own mortality. To understand that it's not the only dangerous one. They get that look in their eyes, and they understand. Fear is a universal language that we all speak, whether we are human, animal or other.

When I struck The Swindler with the blade of the box cutter, he got that look in his eyes.

He pushed me away and ran towards the emergency exit at the back of the gift shop. He leaves a trail of blood behind him, it's spurting out of the front of his chest, and there's so much of it, and it's so glossy and wet, that I almost slip on it as I chase after him.

He leads me out back of the resort and into the woods. Bare trees surround us on both sides, their twisting black branches looming out every which way.

There's still that dense fog in the air. Along with packed snow on the ground that crunches beneath our feet as we run, and a blast of strong wind that pushes us back. I almost lose my balance each time the snowstorm knocks us around. I'm shivering as I pursue him. My teeth chatter in the cold. He's bleeding out profusely.

"Frozen and trembling in the icy snow,

In the severe blast of the horrible wind,

As we run, we constantly stamp our feet,

And our teeth chatter in the cold."

"Winter" By Antonio Vivaldi

I'm still running, my legs are now sharp and throbbing from the intensity of the snow beneath them, with the tingling of blue television static at the base of my feet. The threat of frostbite soon setting in is imminent.

Each time I inhale, I'm gasping in long breaths of freezing air and there's a searing pain inside my lungs. It feels like I've swallowed sharp icicles that prick the inside of my throat and it fucking burns the way dry ice burns when you touch it. I can't run anymore. I'm short of breath and I'm slowing down, I can't keep up with The Swindler, he's way ahead of me now. Why did I think I could chase down a demon, anyway?

He hasn't stopped running even after I've slowed all the way down to a walk and after a few more seconds I've lost sight of him completely. I followed the trail of blood he's left behind in the snow to track him. He's run out of the woods and down a hill, onto a field.

Hot on his heels, I emerged from the woods, from up on top of the hill. I looked down and there he was, far into the distance. There's no trees around him now, it's just a big flat field of snow and nothing else. I can still make out his shrinking silhouette when he finally stumbles and collapses from the massive loss of blood. When he does, there is a loud cracking sound that comes from beneath him. It's the sound of ice breaking. He hasn't run out into a field, no, he's run out onto a frozen lake. He's passed out onto a death trap.

And he's just fallen in. The lake has swallowed him whole.

Some air bubbles up to the surface of where he's fallen through. Then after a little while, the water is still.

When you're drowning in water, you don't appreciate all of the good times that the water has given you: our feet splashing in the pool, swimming with the waves on a summer day at the beach, a relaxing shower. When you are drowning, you only feel the water filling up your lungs, suffocating you, killing you and you resent it. You hate the water. It's turned on you, betrayed you. As your life is being ripped away from you, you'll feel nothing but anger at the senselessness of it all.

I hope he's furious.

CHAPTER EIGHTEEN: SISYPHUS

I trudged my way back to the resort once I was sure that The Swindler had succumbed to an icy, miserable death.

When I walked back in, I was relieved to see that everything was back to normal. It was better than normal, actually. It was thriving. Lush with neon lights and radiant life. Rabid with color. Crowded with people, smiling happy people. People at the bar, full of beer and joy. People at the cafe, in the restaurants, in the shops and at the boutique. Busy hallways, children running around and laughing in the lobby, attentive staff checking new guests in. Filled to the brim with life.

No more sycophants or centipedes. No more Swindler. The resort has been cleansed. I've given it a proper baptism. The casino is so bright inside that it blinds me.

It's been fed very well.

With The Swindler gone for good, I could finally think clearly again. The constant chatter of his voice inside my head is silenced. All I can hear now is the clinking of coins hitting the tray as I sit in front of The Pendulum slot machine. I can finally focus on winning my money back now, forget about everything for a little while and just relax and focus.

The reel spun backwards and it's all the same imagery I've grown accustomed to seeing in the past week, spinning clocks and hourglasses, gems and dollar signs. It spits out little bits of pocket change every few seconds, little breadcrumbs here and there, but never enough to excite me. Never enough to satiate my wallet and get me back into the green. I'm always so close to the jackpot, always one or two away from the big win. So, it's gotta happen soon, it's coming, I know it.

More hours passed by but I still refused to walk out of this place without at least breaking even. I just needed that one big hit, that one major win, to make it all worth it. I've been at the machine all day at this point. I haven't eaten, I ignored anyone who tried to strike up a conversation with me. The Swindler's blood stains have dried up on my shirt. I'm on my own wavelength now, I've tuned the whole world out. I've got tunnel vision on this thing. Nothing matters but winning. I pull the bar down over and over again, I'm bound to the machine.

I'm Sisyphus at the lever.

After a few more hours, another bonus game pops up. But this one is different, it's new. The same sprite that I've seen in the game before appears on screen and smiles.

"Keep playing! You're on a winning streak! Here's a bonus game! Choose the correct three owls to uncover a secret! Good luck!" She rattles off in her computerized, pre-programmed voice and then the screen goes red.

The reel disappears and there are nine owls facing me now, lined up three by three, in the shape of a square. I'm uncertain on how to play the game and pick them, I don't know if I need to press a button or what exactly? Maybe it's a touch screen?

I reached out and touched an owl in the upper right hand corner. Its brown feathers turn gold.

"Great job!" The sprite cheers me on.

Next, I go for the one in the middle to the left. It also turns gold.

"Fantastic!" She squeals with digital delight.

My fingertips are sweaty now. I can feel my heart beating, this is it. C'mon Russell.

I touch the owl in the middle. It turns gold. I hold my breath.

"Amazing!" The sprite congratulates me and continues, but her voice changes. It's not computerized anymore. It's human. Her mannerisms are different now too, no longer robotic, but natural and fluid. She's alive. When she speaks again, it's not the same repetitive sentences I've heard her say over and over. She wasn't reciting the catch phrases anymore, she was expressing new thoughts, actual emotions. She looks directly at me, right into my eyes, and in her human voice she whispers,

"I can tell you the secret now, Russell. You've defeated The Swindler so now you're in control. You can turn back time and get what you really desire. You can reverse the lathe and get Lauren back. All you have to do is hit the jackpot."

Then she looked past me and her soul exited her body. Whatever made her human was gone. She went back to speaking in her electronic, pre-programmed voice.

"Keep playing! You're doing great! You can do this! Your hot streak meter is almost full!"

There was a ghost in the machine.

It's not about the money anymore, the money was now the last thing on my mind. I have to hit the jackpot. I need to get my wife back. I won't leave this place until I have her in my arms again. Until I'm able to take her home with me.

I'm feeding the machine all of the money I have. I'm squeezing blood from a stone. I lose, and lose again. And I keep on losing. Until I hit another win. It's a small win, but it keeps me motivated. And then another loss. A bonus game. A meager win. I'm hit with six more losses in a row and then I realize that I'm starving. How long have I been sitting here? How long have I been pushing this boulder up the hill?

I needed to eat something, I couldn't put it off any longer at this point, it's been days since I've had anything to eat, I haven't had a meal since my visit to the buffet. Just a quick bite. A quick trip to the cafe. Then I'll be back. I'll be right back.

When I stood up, all of my joints ached. My feet were asleep, my whole body was overwhelmingly sore. Muscle atrophy occurs when one goes months without physical activity. It can also happen due to a lack of vitamins, malnutrition and increased age. But I'd only been playing this slot since this morning. Why were my fingernails so long?

At the cafe there's no sign of the redneck. He was one of The Swindler's last victims. It felt weird sitting at the table without him, it didn't seem right. Nothing seems right. I eat my croissant alone, I take a sip of my coffee. They made it fresh with whole beans today. I know he would've liked that.

On the way back to the casino I passed by the upscale boutique.

Their window display was full of precious gemstone jewelry and silk blouses that were draped over lanky headless mannequins. I hadn't noticed the mannequins before but it seemed that today they were calling out to me from the other side of the glass. They were scarecrows that lured people in instead of scaring them away. They were sirens.

I should buy a welcome home gift for Lauren.

Inside the shop, it was full of brightly colored garments. Blouses, dresses and scarves hung on the walls, all made with thread so delicate that even a spider would covet. The fabric was intensely vibrant, it's as if it was purposely created to be overexposed. Clashing patterns of lush flowers, stars and birds adorn each article of clothing, saturated in technicolor hues. Everything in the boutique created a stunning dichotomy, hot pinks on lime greens, blinding and electric, as neon as the casino lights downstairs. The whole room was striking, but not in an awe inspiring way. It was striking in a physical harm kind of way. Harsh on the eyes, like staring into the sun if the sun was jewel toned and covered in floral prints.

All around me, guests flocked about, gazing longingly at the hazardous prints that lined the walls, picking through clothes on the racks, touching the fabric in between their fingers to note the feel and quality of each garment. Blouses, tunics, satin, shirts, silk, scarves, color, color, color, poison, color. Can something be so powerful that it can hurt you just by looking at it? My eyes were starting to burn.

There were two senior ladies in the boutique with me and for some reason, in the dead of winter they both had decided to wear matching Hawaiian shirts and pastel linen shorts. One had sunglasses atop her head, nestled in her short, curly white hair. The other wore blue flip-flops. They looked like the embodiment of Miami, if Miami was a nursing home where tourists go to die.

The ladies were talking amongst themselves and from what I could gather from their conversation, it seemed that they'd just stepped off the bus and arrived at The Lucky Owl this morning. They were quite eager to start their vacation and hit the poker tables, bar and buffet. They had the jittery energy of excited children on Christmas eve, and even in their apparent advanced age they both seemed so much younger than me, but I couldn't explain why.

"Excuse me, ladies," I say to get their attention while holding up two different silk blouses. "My wife has gone away, but she'll be back soon, and I'd like to surprise her with a welcome home gift. Which one should I choose?"

"If you really want to surprise her, you should get her some jewelry. You know, diamonds are forever." says one.

"Yeah, diamonds are forever but so is a shit filled diaper in a landfill." says the other one, cackling.

"Oh shut up, Rose." The first one says in jest, "Don't mind my friend, she's terrible, absolutely terrible." She goes on, "Are you having a good time here? When did you get in?"

"Ah, I've been here about a week now," I pause briefly, "but God, it sure does feel like it's been a lot longer than that."

"I bet," they both laugh, "the reels have a way of hypnotizing you, don't they?"

"Yeah, they've pulled me in, alright. I really miss my wife, I can't wait to get back to her."

"You've got to buy her a necklace! Ooh, look at these ones." They walked over to the display case at the register and I followed behind them.

The cashier behind the case pulled out some necklaces for us to see closer, and I'm immediately drawn to one in particular. It's long and golden with a ruby pendant, Lauren's birthstone.

"What a beauty!" the ladies ooh and aah over it, "your wife is a very lucky gal."

"Well, I hope our luck can turn around soon," I tell them, "fingers crossed."

"Sorry sir," the cashier tells me when I go to pay for the necklace, "your card's been declined."

"That's okay, just put it on my room tab," I shrug like it's no big deal, like I haven't spent my entire life savings in the course of the week I've been here.

"Okay sir, will do. I hope you have a wonderful stay here at The Lucky Owl and thank you for your purpose!" She places the necklace in a shopping bag and hands it to me.

"Excuse me? What did you just say?"

She smiles "I said 'thank you for your purchase!'"

...

At the casino, I pass the other patrons sitting down at the slots, one by one. An elderly man, whose piss soaked diaper pokes out from the back of his pants. A middle aged woman, her hair unbrushed, a frizzled mess, mumbling to herself. An intense man, with sunken in cheeks and a Kubrick stare that's locked onto the reel. I keep on walking past them, paying them no mind.

I approached The Pendulum slot and quickly got right back to playing another round. And then I lose. And lose again. I'm so deep in the red now that it's not even red anymore, it's black. Hours pass and I'm keenly aware that I'm not in control anymore, but I can't do anything about it. All I can do is acknowledge the approaching bankruptcy that is creeping up on me. Another hour passes and I've accrued debts that will be impossible to pay back in my lifetime. Every cent I'll ever make from now on will be garnished from my paycheck and handed over to the casino. I'm destined to live out the rest of my days in a reverse Robin Hood story. I've swiped all of my credit cards dry. And what if I never hit the jackpot? What if I never see her again? Lathes and slot machines are very similar when you think about it- If either one pulls you in, your life is ruined.

If I don't hit the jackpot, I'll have to go back to work. I can never work at that factory again, I can never work at any job again. My only experience is factory work but I don't ever want to step foot inside a factory again. I don't ever want to do anything ever again.

I'll have to work though, I'll still have to work and go grocery shopping and attend social events even though I'm fucking miserable. After a tragedy, you still have to face the world and remain stoic. You have to act like everything is fine. Nobody cares that your wife died, they have their own lives to worry about and you're just another cog in the machine. And if you can't hold it together anymore and you break the facade, if you break down and start cursing at the sky, then you'll lose your job, your house, your standing in the community. You become the homeless man screaming on the corner, the only man who is not acting in this bullshit theater of existence. The man who is truly showing himself to the world, saying "these are my inner thoughts, I'm fully exposed, there's nothing more you can take from me." One must constantly project that they're sane and normal, that they're a functioning human being that is not fully fucking broken on the inside. It's exhausting. Living in this world is fucking exhausting. And Lauren is just the first, I'm going to lose everyone eventually. Everyone I love will die of old age, or cancer, or whatever. The heartless march of time will stomp down every single one of you. No one escapes death. We're all just homeless men screaming on the inside.

I pull the lever and lose again. And again. And again. And again.

A cocktail waitress approaches me, with a tray of drinks in her hand.

"Hi, how are you?" She asks.

"I'm good thanks, how are you?" I smile, like a normal person does.

"I'm fine, thank you. Would you care for a complimentary cocktail?"

"Yes, that would be great. Thank you!"

"Have a good day, sir!"

"Thanks, you too!"

One must imagine Sisyphus happy.

CHAPTER NINETEEN: SOLSTICE

"I don't have any money left to give you. I have nothing left." I say outloud to the machine, defeated. I held my head down and sobbed quietly, my hand still clutching the lever. "All of my credit cards are maxed out. My bank account is empty. I have nothing left, it's gone."

There was a ghost in the machine. And the ghost was possessed by something dark and wrong. And it finally heard me.

My hand melded into the lever, a sticky black substance wrapped around my arm and I quickly realized that I couldn't detach myself from it. It was just one long appendage now, connecting me to the machine, anchoring me down to the entire building. I tried to get my feet against something solid so that I could push away. Nothing was in reach and the harder I kicked, the tighter the machine grasped at my hand, as if I had angered it.

And in its anger I could feel the blood in my arm pulsating hot against its electric currents.

A dance of voltage and wires and veins.

I panicked and struggled against this fucking thing until I had completely depleted all of my energy. Until it had exhausted me fully. No one around me noticed. They were all trapped inside their own prisons that were disguised as reveries of riches and jackpots. They were empty shells, zombies with dollar signs in their eyes, forever entranced by the reels in front of them. They had already surrendered themselves over, and I was next.

"Feed the machine or perish," the sprite demands.

With its reel, the machine began to drain the blood from my body, the only valuable thing I had left. I slumped over and went limp. I couldn't keep my head up any longer, I was light headed, in an absolute daze. My vision was fuzzy, I was seeing double and the room spun around me. There was a gathering blackness that surrounded the corners of my eyes. I'm nauseous, I'm going to throw up all over my lap because I'm too weak to lift my head up, it's completely numb now. My one hand that is not attached to the lever is cold and clammy. Everything is cold and clammy. I can't breathe. There's the taste of copper in my mouth, on my tongue, behind my teeth. The sounds are fading out around me. I feel something hard bash into the side of my forehead. I'm slipping in and out of consciousness when an overwhelming sense of calm washes over me. This is it. This is how I die. I'm almost completely gone from this world when the machine lights up and blinks with big red letters-

"CONGRATULATIONS. YOU'VE UNLOCKED THE SCATTER FEATURE."

The pendulum swung around wildly, violently knocking against the edges of the screen until it cracked from within. The images of vibrant gems and dollar signs that I've grown accustomed to seeing on the reels had been suddenly replaced with strange, otherworldly symbols that I didn't recognize. They had never appeared before, and now they were popping up all over the screen. The whole machine illuminated like a fluorescent inferno, blinking and flashing with an intense red strobe that could only be described as belonging on a dance floor in a nightclub that was situated in the depths of hell. A danger to the eyes.

More and more symbols appeared on the reel, ancient sigils scattered all over the screen, dancing and spinning around, until they had completely covered the reels and screen entirely.

The speakers on each side of the screen wailed out "JACKPOT! JACKPOT! JACKPOT! JACKPOT! JACKPOT! JACKPOT!" and throbbing beats screamed in succession.

The machine pumped all of the blood that was inside of it back into me and a rush of coins fell out of its slot, clinking and clanking against the tray on the way down. They continued to tumble out, a golden cascade of prosperity. There was a heap of gold coins next to me now, piling up to my knees with no signs of slowing down. The blood circulated and flowed throughout my body, until every one of my senses was heightened. I don't even think that it was just my blood, it was more than just mine, I must have had the blood of a dozen others coursing through my veins right now and I had never felt so powerful. So invigorated.

The reel that still had a full hold on my arm finally released me, then I felt something different hold me from behind with both hands. A familiar hold. A loving embrace.

It was Lauren.

She held on to me so tightly, as if she was never going to let go of me again.

I turned around and there she was. It was really her. Everything is good. Everything has a purpose. There is a God and He did have a plan for me. I could feel Him pulsating inside of my veins. Lauren was standing there, in front of me, in the flesh. I marveled at the sight of her. A miracle had taken place. God had acknowledged me directly.

I'm in control now and I have everything I want. I had the strength of a dozen men and the ability to manipulate time to get her back. And now she's back. I got her back. She hugged me and I held her tighter than I ever have before. Her eyes were as beautiful as the day I met her. She was warm and happy and so alive. So god damn alive, so full of life.

"We can go home now," I tell her.

She smiles, "I know!"

"God, I've missed you so much."

"I never thought I'd see you again. It feels so amazing to be back."

"It feels right. It feels like it should be. Everything is going to be okay."

"I can't believe you won, babe. You really did it, you actually hit the jackpot!" She laughs, her eyes well up with tears. Mine do too.

"Let's go home."

Everything is wonderful and meaningful and pure.

…

Lauren and I have been home for about a week now. We've settled back in as if nothing had changed because it hadn't, really. I had her back and that's all that mattered. We cleaned up the whole place, put away the heaps of funeral flowers, did the laundry that had accumulated on the floor and washed the pile of dishes in the sink. We wiped the counters and sprayed enough bug spray to take down a horse.

Lauren was ready to face the world again, but I don't think the world was ready to face her. Not yet. We talked about moving, starting new somewhere, and easing her family into this strange, new reality where she existed again. I wanted so badly to tell them about The Lucky Owl and the things that I had experienced, the powers of the resort, but where would I even begin? Would they even believe it was really her?

It's early Christmas morning now and we're in our living room, sitting together on the couch. The television is on, and 'It's A Wonderful Life' is playing. Our tree is in the corner, with unwrapped gifts underneath it. We couldn't wait until Christmas Day to open them. Lauren loved the KitchenAid mixer the most out of everything. There's coffee brewing in the kitchen and the cheerful sounds of the neighbors racing down the street in their new sled; metal blades gliding across snow, children laughing, with their barking dog chasing after them. We keep our curtains closed.

"Maybe we should get a dog too."

"We absolutely should. Like a golden retriever?"

"Hmm, I was thinking more like a black lab."

"Yeah, that would be really nice. My friend had a black lab when we were growing up, it followed us everywhere we went. I think it was a birthday present."

"Oooh, speaking of birthdays, I can't wait to try out my new mixer. The first thing I want to make is a cake for Emma's birthday party."

"Emma?"

"Yeah, Stacey's daughter."

"Oh right. Aw man, her birthday is right after Christmas? That's a bummer. How are they doing? Uh, I'm assuming you'll send the cake anonymously? Or through a service or something?"

Lauren answers my first two questions but ignores the last two.

"They're good. Emma just started girl scouts and she really likes it. Stacey has been texting everyone about buying girl scout cookies, she's kinda relentless about it too. I mean, I'll buy them, but I don't want to feel peer pressured into doing it, you know?"

"Wait, have you been in contact with them? I thought you were just going to watch them from afar for now on social media, like we had talked about. We're not ready to re-introduce you to everyone yet, they wouldn't understand."

She laughs, "Hey, are you hungry?" then asks me, "What should I make for breakfast? Eggs or pancakes? Or eggs and pancakes? Let's have a big Christmas breakfast, I'm starving. Russell, Russell? He's waking up, he's moving, doctor! Get the doctor!"

She stares off in a daze and I rush over to her,

"What?? Lauren, honey, what are you saying?" Oh fuck, could this be some kind of after effect for bringing her back to life? Is she glitching out? Cursed?

She continues, her eyes still blank and distant. "You're at St. Johns. Don't worry, everything is alright. It's mom. Can you hear me?"

I shake her to try to get her to snap out of it, "Lauren! Lauren?"

But then I'm not at home anymore, I'm laying down on a bed. There's an I.V. hooked up to my arm. My mouth is dry and my eyes are crusted over. My body feels light but heavy at the same time.

129

The weakness you experience after coming out of a blackout. The Christmas tree is gone. There is no children's laughter or dogs barking coming from outside. No bells are rung, and no angels get their wings. My family surrounds me, her family too, but no sight of her.

"Lauren! Where's Lauren? What's going on?"

"Russell, you're in the hospital. You had a seizure." My father tells me while pointing at my forehead, "You bumped your head pretty hard and you've been out since last night."

"Where's Lauren?"

"Lauren is dead. She died last month." Her brother tells me.

"No. She came back. I brought her back. I won."

"Russell, honey, Lauren is gone, she's not coming back. I'm so sorry." My mom tries to explain.

"What? No? She was just here."

My sister sighs, "Listen, Russell. Take your jackpot money and go see a therapist, you know? You can probably afford the best ones out there now with all of the money you won. Start going to some grief counseling sessions or something. We all care about you, but you need help."

"Jackpot money?"

"Yeah, you hit the jackpot," she let out a quiet laugh and I could feel the tension in the room lift a little.

"You hit the jackpot and then went out cold. It must've been all the flashing lights. Have you been taking your epilepsy medication?"

My mom asked.

"No, I guess I forgot to pack it. I forgot to pack all of my medication. How much did I win?"

Lauren's brother held up the check to show me. He grinned, but his eyes remained somber. Everyone in the room had the same expression as he did. Celebratory but sad for me at the same time. Smiles that didn't reach their eyes.

It was a ridiculously huge amount, the biggest amount of money that I had ever seen on a single check.

I don't have the heart to tell them that it doesn't even come close to what I had spent to get it, I didn't even break even. I put more money in that fucking machine than I ever got back out of it.

I didn't win anything. The only thing I gained was an addiction.

CHAPTER TWENTY: SUNRISE

In the mirror that hangs on the wall at the therapist's waiting room, the swollen bump on my forehead reflects back at me. It resembles the color and texture of a rotting pomegranate, lumpy and bruised dark from old blood that has clotted to the surface. A week later and it's still sore from the fall. The doctor at the hospital told me that I had a concussion and might be out of it for a while. He told me that I fell out of my chair at the casino when the jackpot lights went off. I don't remember much of it. Everything feels cloudy and distant; it's been hard to recollect any of my time at the resort, it's been hard to articulate my words or form new thoughts. It's been hard to do anything lately.

The entire essence of 'you' as you understand it is one blocked blood vessel, one head injury, or a few wrongly folded proteins away from regressing into a completely different person. An impaired person, one who may never fully be right again. Intellectual disability, anger issues, memory loss, chronic migraines, and tinnitus are all common symptoms people report after a traumatic brain injury. Sometimes, the symptoms go away. Sometimes, they don't.

It's hard to wrap your head around such a depressing concept. We are ultimately the product of a squishy computer made of meat and our concept of self requires it not getting fucked up. Which was bad news for me. If your body is a temple, a brick has been thrown through the window of mine.

While waiting to see the therapist, I tried to think of what to tell her when she called me in. Where to even start. After a traumatic event it's odd what your mind decides to retain, like the pattern on a stranger's shirt or the song that was playing on the radio. Those small details are a part of you now. A core memory. And now, every time you hear that song, every time you see that pattern, the trauma comes rushing back. My short term memory was pretty fucked from the concussion, but the day that Lauren died replays in my mind even when nothing else can. When you're in your head too much, you're not experiencing the outside of it, you're not living in the present. That is what grief is, holding on to the past. The worst part is, it doesn't follow any kind of order. You can be depressed one minute, then hopeful, then angry, then depressed again. Most people think of the seven stages of grief as a designated timeline that goes straight from one stage to the next until you reach acceptance and can graduate from your suffering. But grief is not a line, it's not linear. It's a circle. It's a circle that spins like a lathe, a slot machine, a ballerina in a music box, a CD in a CD player that plays Christmas music over and over, a cake mixer...

"Russell, Doctor Pelling will see you now."

Her office was decorated in calming hues and comfortable furniture. Light blue pillows and chairs, soft lighting. A box of tissues on the table next to a little toy train, with a tiny gnome as its conductor. Affirmations of support and encouragement hung in picture frames above her head. An exotic palm leaf plant was nestled in the corner. I shifted anxiously in my seat as I explained the last few weeks to her.

"The next day after Lauren's death" I began, "I woke up and I couldn't believe the sun was shining. Our friends shared pictures of themselves online, eating out at nice restaurants or going on vacation. Our neighbors played catch with their children outside of our window. Strangers celebrated their birthdays and got married. Didn't they know the most amazing woman had died? I wanted the world to stop and for everyone to feel like I did. It seemed unreal that something so life changing had happened but everyone continued on as normal except me. I'm still in shock. Nothing feels right, I can't even differentiate between what's real life and what's a dream anymore, especially now, after my concussion."

Dr. Pelling is soft-spoken in a soothing way, like she's trying to cushion me with her words and gently ease me into the session.

"Shock is scary because nothing feels real, but it is real. It will take a while for your brain to accept that this terrible thing has happened. Your brain is trying to protect you, it wants you to forget the brutality you faced on that day, it wants you to think that Lauren is still alive. Russell, do you know what Post Traumatic Stress is? It's what you're experiencing. Allow yourself to grieve, to cope. Allow your brain to rest. You are dealing with a lot and it's okay to take it one day at a time. These are normal reactions to a very non-normal situation. When you're feeling overwhelmed, you can do a mindfulness exercise to ground yourself. Focus on three things to see, two things to hear and one thing to touch."

Everything repeats itself. I've done this song and dance before.

"Right now I can't focus on anything. I keep replaying that day in my mind. I had just gotten back from my lunch break. There was blood everywhere, I still remember the smell. My boss was wearing a plaid shirt. At her funeral, someone gifted me a big hardcover book about losing a loved one. I could hardly get out of bed or dress myself, let alone tackle a 400 page manual on how I should feel. It felt good to throw it across my room though."

"It's okay to not be okay. To feel angry or frustrated. It's okay to feel lonely, to feel anxious or confused."

"I just want to feel normal again."

"How are you feeling right now?"

"I feel detached. Distant. Like everything is floating and I can't anchor myself down. Like I can't tether myself to anything."

"You may be feeling that way because of the concussion. Are you having any other symptoms?"

"A dull headache that won't go away, a mild dizziness that comes and goes, and just a lot of tinnitus."

"These are all normal after a concussion. It's common to feel dizzy or hear a ringing in your ears. It should go away in a few more days but let me know if things get worse."

"Lauren always helped me when I wasn't at my best. She took care of me when I was sick. She made sure I took my medication, and always found it when I would accidentally misplace it. She was always so good at finding little things I would lose around the house, like pencils or keys. Right after her death, I lost the television remote under a pile of junk. I know it's a small thing, but it was just one more reminder of how lost I am without her. I don't know what to do. Her funeral was a closed casket and I never got to say goodbye."

"How about you write her a letter? Write her a letter and tell her how you feel. Say goodbye to her. I think that's something that you need to do."

...

Back home, in my kitchen, I'm rummaging through my fridge for a late night snack. Even though I was only out of town for about a week and a half, when I came home, all of the food in my fridge had gone bad. All the perishable stuff had rotted, the fruits and vegetables. The casseroles that were brought over by well-meaning relatives had grown green and moldy. Even the yogurt that shouldn't have expired for another month had gone sour. When I first opened the door, the smell of rotten meat smacked me in the face. It was an overbearing odor of rancid, curdled fat and spoiled flesh. I've made three different grocery runs since I got back but everything keeps expiring so quickly, even the food I just bought yesterday has already gone bad. I think my fridge must be broken. I stopped looking for a snack and headed to bed.

In my bedroom, cobwebs had collected on the ceilings, and thick dust coated along the windowsill and on all of the furniture. It seemed like every shirt I pulled out of my dresser had moth holes in it. When I opened my mail all of it had aged weirdly, yellowed and brittle, as if it had been sitting in the mailbox for years. The rest of the house was covered in dust and cobwebs as well. It was going to take some real effort to clean it all, and I just didn't have it in me right now.

My bed seemed normal enough, thankfully. I turned on a fan and when my tinnitus finally quieted down a bit, I was able to drift off to dreamland.

I'm in the breakroom at the factory, it's just as I remember it, even the vending machine is in the right place. The rest of the building is empty, as far as I can tell, there are no supervisors or coworkers around. There is a piece of paper on the breakroom table with a pen next to it. The top of the paper is titled "A Goodbye Letter" and the rest of it is blank. I sit down and start to write.

"Dear Lauren, I love you and will always love you. I miss you so much, I

physically ache with you not here anymore. We were supposed to grow old together. Things weren't meant to happen this way, but they did. I have to accept that you're gone, Lauren. I can't change it, I can't go back and make things different. I have to accept the truth, I have to start facing reality. God, I miss you so much, I would do anything to have you back but there's nothing that can be done. I'll always love you and that will never change."

I leave the necklace that I bought for her from The Lucky Owl boutique on the table, along with the letter. I hope she's able to find it somehow, in another dimension or parallel universe, an afterlife perhaps. In another space and time that she might be occupying. Maybe one day I will occupy it too. I don't know if I believe in heaven anymore, but I believe that she's out there, somewhere, and maybe we'll see each other again when my time comes.

When I awoke, I felt at peace. That feeling lasted until my memories of the resort came back.

CHAPTER TWENTY ONE: SUNSET

"I need to tell you about what I experienced," I told Dr. Pelling. It's our next therapy session together.

"I'm starting to remember my time at the casino and I need to talk about it."

"Good. That's a good sign. I'm glad to hear that your memories are coming back."

I take a deep breath, "the resort, there was something strange about it. There was a man who followed me. He had powers. The resort had powers."

"Whoa. Slow down." Dr. Pelling looked concerned.

"I don't know how to explain it, I know I sound crazy. But I saw things. This man, he had control over people, they followed me, they wanted me."

"Why would they be following you? What did you have that they wanted?"

"It doesn't make any sense to say it aloud. But the man, he wanted my hearing."

"You're right, Russell. That doesn't make any sense. Do you have a history of mental illness, of experiencing delusions? You didn't mention anything like this in your paperwork or at our last session."

"Yes, but, no, but I- I know what I saw was real. I've had a mental break before, I even had another therapist before you, back when I was attending art school. But this was different, this was not like my past delusions. I know the difference."

I tried to tell her about The Swindler, and what he was capable of. What he did to those people, his victims. But the more I talked, the more I realized that that's all they were. Delusions. A temporary case of psychosis, brought on by profound grief and sleepless nights. She was right. I needed to get back on my medications. She smashed every single thing I told her against the rocks of reality until I had conceded.

"Russell, I think we should get you to the psychiatrist. We need to update you on your medications."

"The Swindler felt so real, I saw others interacting with him. I saw him at the casino games, betting on black jack, and poker and roulette."

"While the man might've been a real person, the delusions you were having about him were not real."

"I remember now, I was in the casino's basement, and I was stuck there, for a thousand years it seemed. I couldn't escape. I don't know how I survived. It broke the laws of reality, I didn't need to eat or sleep. I didn't age but my mind worked constantly, it never stopped. I was alone with my thoughts for an eternity. It was torture. I was tortured. Maybe they were just my delusions, but the pain I suffered was real."

"Russell, I'm going to write you a referral to the psychiatrist in this office building. He can help you. Besides your emotional state, how are you feeling, physically? Have the symptoms from your concussion improved?"

"Everything feels okay, no more headaches or dizziness. Except for the tinnitus, the tinnitus is getting worse. There's always a buzzing in my ears now, it won't go away." It's so bad that it's hard to fall asleep at night."

"I'll talk to the psychiatrist and see if he can get you on a sleeping aid prescription for that as well. You're going to get better. Try not to think about the man or the resort, okay? Let's focus on something positive before we end our session. Did you write the letter to Lauren yet?"

"Yes actually. Weirdly enough, I didn't write it in real life. I wrote it in a dream I had. I know that might not count, but my dreams have felt so real lately, and when I woke up, I felt better for a little while."

"That's good, I think that counts. It's a start, at least. Writing the letter is the beginning of your journey towards closure, the beginning of your healing process. We want to eventually move towards acceptance, but that is a long way away. It takes time, a lot of time. Once you get there, to that finish line, you'll be able to heal and move forward. One day at a time. You are stronger than you think. Acceptance is the last stage of grief and you will get there."

CHAPTER TWENTY TWO: BUST

"The goal of blackjack is to get the closest to 21 without going over. If you go over, you lose. It's called a bust." That sentence popped into my head earlier today. I say it again, outloud this time, but I don't know why. I remember saying it at the casino while I was watching a man play at the blackjack table. Just a man, not The Swindler. The Swindler wasn't real. I'm back on my medications and I can't believe how far gone I had gotten. How bad I had let myself get. The Swindler was just a man that I had projected all of my fears and insecurities onto.

My phone rang, it was the police again. I answered it this time. I hadn't been necessarily avoiding them on purpose, I was just avoiding everyone right now. It was hard to hear anything over the tinnitus, the incessant buzzing in my ears, a high pitched dial tone that I couldn't hang up. It was getting louder every day, so I just stopped talking to people altogether.

"Hello, This is Officer Weber. Is this Russell Clark?"

"Hi, yes it is."

"Hey Russell. I've been trying to get a hold of you…"

"I'm sorry," I cut him off, "I've been really sick."

"You need to come to the station and review some things regarding your wife's death. If you don't come now, we'll have to send an officer to pick you up."

"No, that won't be necessary. I'm on my way."

The interrogation room is a stark contrast to a therapist's room, even though you're supposed to reveal your deepest secrets in both. It's just an empty white room, with no decorations, no pictures, plain uncomfortable metal chairs with a cold metal table to match. No distractions, no comforting items to soothe you. This is where they get people to confess. This is where they break people. I don't know why I was here.

"You're not in trouble." The officer tells me as he wheels in a cart with a laptop on it. A few other officers follow behind him, and a detective, I think.

"Your boss was checking over the security footage from the day that your wife died. He saw something that he couldn't explain and emailed the video to us. Maybe you can explain it, maybe you know something he doesn't?"

He clicked the laptop's keyboard a few times and a video started. It's the security footage, but the accident hadn't taken place yet. The factory was empty and the camera zoomed in with a birds eye view on the lathe and its surroundings. I could see the breakroom to the left, and some other equipment and machinery to the right. It's quiet. I notice the date in the corner of the footage. It's the correct date, the day my life changed forever.

As the footage plays, a man emerges from the breakroom. He's tall and lanky, with ruffled hair and a pointed nose. He's holding a piece of paper in one hand and a necklace in the other. It's him. It's The Swindler.

"Your boss doesn't recognize this man, says he doesn't work there. Do you recognize him?"

"You can see him?" I point to him on the laptop screen, "you can see him too?"

There's a resounding 'yes' from everyone in the room.

We all watch as The Swindler walks over to the lathe, pulls a piece of gum from his mouth and uses it to stick the piece of paper to the back of the machine. I recognize the paper. It's the goodbye letter I wrote to Lauren in my dream just days ago. He then lays the necklace I bought for her out on a worktable near the lathe, with a gift tag tied around it. I can barely make out the words that are written on the tag, but I'm sure it says "To Lauren, From Russell." He walks to the exit and slips out of the building, unnoticed. When Lauren walks into the room a few minutes later, she sees the necklace. She smiles and puts it on, tucking it under her shirt collar.

The tinnitus in my head grows louder. The officers start asking me questions but I can't hear them. The security footage keeps playing.

We see Lauren inspecting the metal tube that is locked into the lathe. The lathe is off. She is wearing safety goggles and a form fitting work shirt, as is company procedure. When she turns the motor on, the headstock begins to spin. A cutting tool is grasped firmly in her hand, she goes to move it towards the spinning metal, but then pauses and puts the tool down. She walks closer to the left of the lathe and reaches over, it seems that something has caught her attention from behind the security camera's view. It's the letter I wrote to her, she must recognize my handwriting. As she reaches around to get a better look, the long chain necklace she just put on, falls out from under her shirt, which was previously tucked inside her collar. It lands directly onto the moving spindle.

The officer shuts the laptop closed before it can go any further. Him and the other officers continued to ask me questions but I couldn't hear them, I can't hear anything now. I can only hear the constant noise in my head and it's just getting louder. The officers are shouting at me now, they lean in closer to me until they all surround me, and insist that I answer their questions. Demand that I speak to them. But they're all so distant, their voices are so distant. The tinnitus is not going away, it's never going away. I can't answer anything they ask me. The high pitched buzz that only I can hear is deafening. It's a tone that would drive anyone mad. It fills my head completely and I'm powerless to it.

The Swindler told me that there was a sound that only the dying could hear. And now I know what that sound is.

It's the sound of rows and rows of overhead fluorescent lights. All buzzing at a constant.

The police are gone. The detective is gone. The room is now covered in yellowed wallpaper. The floor below me is a faded green, it's the color of an old poker table that had been left out in the sun and abandoned years ago. There's a hole in the ceiling. A large gray rock falls from it and drops in front of me.

"Where their worm does not die, and the fire is not quenched." Mark 9:48

Printed in the USA
CPSIA information can be obtained
at www.ICGtesting.com
LVHW071147080524
779548LV00002B/304